i cope.

CCM edition made possible in collaboration with author and press.

CCM Design & Cover by *Michael J Seidlinger*

ISBN – 978-0-9846037-1-8

Support experimental fiction, and the Other.

Join our community and find yourself

through innovative fiction

a coping mechanism perfect for your needs.

http://copingmechanisms.net

SUNSHINE in the VALLEY

Kyle Muntz

I

Sunshine in the Valley

We grew wings for the afternoon; we tore a path through the flowers. Bare feet on damp wet grass, the sound of singing. Landscape cut a profile, melding laughter and sunflower seeds, shadows and joy. We played all day in the hills, until the real dark came. Faces turned red from exhaustion, from running. Hands lofted dandelions as gifts to the wind. Naked fields and a bright flaming eye, the sunrise screaming. Jacob rolled into a patch of goldenrod; Laura prayed for nature; Gidian sang songs about morning.

Far away stood the walls, tall shadows falling from them, hard stone containing. Blue firmament embraced us. The trees gave little shade, but cast monovalent twins, sharp lines twining below. Wild orchids grew, rustled by the only breeze in the entire world. Laura blessed them. Jacob swung his arms. Gidian gave lessons in perspective.

We came here once a day, as the sun opened full in the sky. It was the highest point in the village, the very center of the valley, and the days were blinking passage for us, always to glorious burning. No adult had set foot here for a million days; sometimes we heard stories, in which memory bound them to smallness, but not the timelessness we knew. We were here and we were really here. It kept us breathing.

We formed a circle, holding hands, and Laura spoke of flowers, whispering secrets, freeing spirits encased. Each held a soul, folded within a womb of petals, suspended upon equidistant bridges of light, an infinitesimal universe. The light got through—a great, radiant halo of light—magnified to no measurable proportion, etching statues in whitewashed space, weaving a contralto array of voices, meshing as the wind slipped through it.

She taught us laughter, Gidian said. *She was*
with us in the morning.

::::::::::::::::::

Unclimbable walls surround us. They have many shapes—gray bricked patterns of stones, granite tumblings, the slate heft of a gigantic mountain—and morph incessantly between them, emitting the low growl of churning earth. At the base is a clear stretch of uncertain length, gravel wastes lifted occasionally by the shifting walls.

Many climb when shallow inclines appear, but the wall is as unfeeling as it is tall, unreachable as the clear blue sky. Making no distinction between itself and the outside, a tempestuous grasp comes for them, liquid shifts in the sodium gratings, and they become a part of that metamorphic fluid, seemingly swallowed. Death leaves no scar as new skin closes over. Choosing to jump, a few survive, but not often—and might even be caught in the fall, upon a surging platform like outstretched hands.

Our village spreads among the hills. There we grow vegetables and all variety of flowers. Modest housing sets at an angle for lack of even space, and paths lead through gaps in the foliage. Grass grows sweet and short. Scents of blooming drift a copious body.

Midday ushers unparalleled beauty. Light banishes harsh shadows; brightness dances in the garden. Men and women work them, taking frequent breaks—in fact breaking breaks to work, more often walking together amongst many pathways, past whole families picnicking on fine soft blankets, children playing wherever they choose. The sun holds its place at the center of the sky, greeting each morning as it opens a xanthous eye. Spreading brightness moves to its peak in amplitude; semblance becomes an aspect of vision.

There are many children in the village, but the hill is open only to us. Others sneak there, but find themselves severely punished. They'll always wonder what we see, even if we can't explain it. Our ritual has been tradition for thousands upon thousands of days (upon thousands). We function as an extension of the past, molding now to then, continuously reliving. The birthing day opens its arms to us. Sunshine finds a home in the valley.

Our village has a legend of the (nameless) Sun God and his journey to earth. He planted a garden here, a single seed, and all life sprang from it. Lush vines and bright blooming. When he finished planting he took a step back, then returned to his temple in the center of the sky, and opens his eye each day to look at us, so that he might give us his light, and we might please him by being.

Our village has many legends. Almost all of them involve the sun.

::::::::::::::::::::

Jacob's father was a priest of the Sun God. The only one. Most days he spent walking through the village, looking to the altar. His study smelled of mystery; his library held many books. Children feared him, Jacob most of all, though he couldn't tell sometimes where fear ended and more complicated things began. His father was very old; bore heavy hands laced with pale blue veins; a face creased and tall and proud. As priest, for responsibility to himself, to others, he spoke to his son of mythology, and fed him with stories.

::::::::::::::::::::

Metamorphosis blasted a vertical landscape. The cliff changed from purple to gray, mincing composition, its obstacle face distorting. Geysers arched, froze, and became sculptured fountains; gushed backwards, disjointing presence.

Hung shadows cast craved engravings.

At the base, the rock had none of these properties, but its roughness cut the tips of Jacob's fingers. He wore supplies, and boots, but they were much too heavy. Having fallen many times at their expense, he let them go.

A heavy thump sounded below, nearly drowned by the roar above. The climb was difficult, if not impossible, but he'd scarcely left the ground.

At a height perhaps twice his own, a vice closed around his ankle. That hand belonged to his father. It led back to his father's arm, shoulder, and face, all in hideous combination—

And then Jacob was falling.

He landed with a lateral crash, bruising a shoulder; then felt himself lifted to his feet, by a cloaked shadow—and those same hands slapped Jacob twice. The second blow might have knocked the boy to the ground, but he was lifted midway, to be borne roughly in the direction of the village: odd transitions, galaxy distension, invisible stars.

He and his father never spoke of the day. It had been long ago, so long Jacob ceased to count, after a hundred days... five hundred... a thousand. For all his aura of intimidation the man was fair—but not kind, never that—and Jacob didn't know if he resented him for the violence or thanked him for waking him up. Not that he had words for either.

More and more he thought of this—more and more he wanted to forget. The village was his first love, his *only* love. It was where he'd been born, where he belonged; and he feared the outside, the distant, the strange.

That night his father spoke more than ever of story, as though to supplement their nameless abscess, invisible geometries between them. Grated voice and the firelight: Jacob sat on the floor too late at night, legs tucked beneath him, hands and arms together. Though negligent in conversation—his father partook of very few, and said little or nothing even then—within these sessions a cough became apparent, and a weak, raspy quality to the voice.

Having lived this life, Jacob knew many legends, yet he had nothing of the teller in him. At night, he looked out the window across his bed. He hid them in a secret cave upon shelves made of diamond, afraid to let them out—and no light seeped in, but he pretended to see something of its shape, a follower in dreams.

Tales have many shapes, and like the walls they are never the same. We have only one god but he appears as man, as woman, as many. The sun is such an element of our culture as to *become* our culture. We speak, think, ponder it constantly; draw our symbolism from it; interpret and measure experience, vilifying the things we see.

For the most part Jacob wore his father's old clothes; without exception, they fit perfectly. Unlike the other boys, who had mothers to make clothes for them, to sew them shut, to pull and thread the fibers, his clothes were old, and older than any he'd ever seen: they had holes, the color long faded, creases become permanent amongst the many tears. His father never spoke of her, and he and his son were identical, excepting drastic differences in age. So similar they might have been the same person.

But even now, especially now, Jacob couldn't help remembering that day he'd almost climbed; feeling he'd kept too many secrets, so far down they weren't his anymore (might *never* have been his), at the bottom of himself, a haven of monsters, and even though he'd stayed behind, something else, a part of him, might have already gone—or been lost in hiding.

Jacob spent much time with other children, often eating dinner with other families, who never ceased to amaze him for how similar they were—not to his family, but to everyone else's. Perhaps they were more prone to laughter, kindling bigger, warmer fires, but even those were just other elements of the valley in rearrangement, a path lain by eons of ancestors. They live on in us, and we keep them alive, truly.

Late at night, he liked to go exploring. As a rule neighbors confined themselves to their own homes, if they could stay awake at all. Jacob's father held strict rules, and he couldn't risk getting caught. Nights heralded absolute darkness. No abeyance hung in the sky, rendering the world invisible. It was a secondary village, hidden within the first— overlaying the same space, same places—that had different rules, where hidden places knew secrecy. He carried a lamp but never lit it until he went far beyond the gardens: ember of flame, dancing in a container of glass.

"Are you here?" he asked.

"I'm here."

::::::::::::::::::::

Laura was a harbinger of petals. Autumn enmeshed her, energy flowing away. She spent her life in the gardens. Her furnace. Hyacinth and lilac, pinkness, a gradual reaching for the sky, each striving onward, upward, toward the apotheosis of the sun, nutrient wisdom tethering life to living. In her hand death became green again. Where things grew she felt them, saw them. Hazing motes, rising from brush and flowers.

::::::::::::::::::

He hadn't thought she'd come, but she came.

She shivered, so he gave her his coat. It looked understandably shabby, but no one saw, no one *could* see. Pebbles rustled, and the night banished all scent. Icy sheets of merciless blackness. A gaping sky fell around them.

Jacob found himself still mesmerized by the lamp. In all possibility, at this moment, it cast the only illumination in all the world—not light, in the context he knew, but an imitation, an *abomination* of it. Real light possessed a two way seeing, a sign of the Sun God's presence and blessing, who forbade a lamp in all but the direst circumstances. Those circumstances never came.

They found no paths this far out, but thin grasses grew. Jacob felt himself one of two occupants of the known universe, this narrow flickering universe, that might be extinguished in an instant. The dark didn't scare him, but he understood what it meant to be alone—in fact fed on oneness, especially now, that he might share it. In a sense one was always alone. Nothing had ever been together.

The wastes opened to them. This place was said to be dangerous, but Jacob came here every night amidst worship: a desert king, circling the world in less time than it took to walk through it; or the world moved around him.

Infrequently they came upon a boulder, lodged like a severed tooth.

"Last night," Laura said, "I had a dream about this. It's why I came. Or else I wouldn't have. I didn't want to."

What happened?

"There was a phoenix," she said, awakening in stone. It spread granite wings, peering with eyes made of fire. Below, two figures linked hands, dressed exactly as they were now, watching the birth of the phoenix, except it took place at day—grown brighter, beneath blazing wings.

"What did we do?"

"You held my hand," she said, "as the phoenix came." It changed from blue to green to orange. The carving glowed dimmer, emblem to its great pinioned counterpart. A waver in space and it came to them below, bearing its neck beside the hill in the center of the valley, no village, nor even gardens, but only a plane of finely hewed grasses.

Jacob didn't know it, but he squeezed her hand very tightly.

"And then we rode it over the wall together," she said, "just you and me."

"Did it burn?"

"No," she said. "It was like a fire made of flowers."

:::::::::::::::::::

Despite his assurance, they kept the wall at the distance of a thrown stone. Jacob created a path ahead. Laura wore a thin gown and his aforementioned additions, still shivering despite the gentle night.

From this distance the wall subtly glowed—but the glow wasn't on the surface, he saw *into* the rock, a flood of energy inside. Purple pinkish to aqua menagerie. Hues like interpretations of a fine song, channeled through many mediums. The audio, the visual, the genuine. A wind flowing in it. The drip dripping percolation. A need to brace: strong face in the silence.

"When I was very young," Jacob said, "my father showed this place to me. He told me we didn't have anything to be afraid of, but that I should never come here again." They'd come during the day, but as the sun shut its eye—no explosion, only a gradual dimming of celestial tones, blue to darker blue, rarely a hint of orange. He didn't know why he remembered.

"I came here with my mother," Laura replied, "when she was still making my sister. She said she wanted her to see the world—" as she knew it, the circular, diagonal, reptilian world—"so we came."

"After he told me that," Jacob said, "I tried to climb."

"Why?

"I don't know."

"If you came back, it wouldn't be you anymore."

Jacob bore tunnels in the walls. He witnessed their glowing.

"Yeah," he said. "I know."

::::::::::::::::::::

The cave might have been invisible without the lantern, but Jacob shined the beam inside, igniting presence. Nothing moved beyond ranges of vision. Living in the village meant connection to the sky. Inside were new boundaries and frames of being; staggering alterations to consciousness.

Light washed the walls. Cracks ran like age in ancient skin, crumbling blocks impaled beside. Discontinuity snaked the length, stone jutted above and below. They walked carefully though the path was clear, at any moment expecting change, petrification, strangulation. When the door closed no air would come to them. If they could move, if they *were*, it would be a wait to choke on spoiled breath, really truly the only ones in a small cold universe, kept expanded by belching specks in the oil.

Energy moved above and below. Fragmenting waveforms, undulating geofront planes, spangled electricity: prisms reflected in rainbows, storming unreal. Particle beams refracted in the latches.

True new glaciers level mountains. So sang melting glass.

Such inception until they came to a chamber. The walls broke upwards; myriad ornaments lay in welcome. The room wasn't large, but the cave went no further. There was no door in the far wall, but a painting of one so detailed there might have been. Old emblems collected little dust; in fact collected none, no oxidation, no appearance of rotting. Everything was flat here: a temple of flatness.

He studied a carving against one wall: three marks filled deeply with ink, two curving towards some invisible point of interconnection, the third negating the first. It held rough edges; angles convex and concave. In the village everything important was white, whereas black encompassed perversion in its vile fullness of body—suggesting strains of rebellion and newness; abandonment of rounded edges (by similitude of shape, a likeness to the sun); an unwillingness to distinguish direction: very prominent, irreversible. The wetness of the paint disputed its apparent age.

Other objects bore an unfamiliar language, but proximity revealed that they weren't objects at all; everything in the *room* was painted. A low table displayed a golden urn, bedecked in spidery characters. Nearby hung pictures, and fragments of a story; an empty cage against the far wall.

::::::::::::::::::

Laura dangled loosely in her body, her figure collapsing—skin of pale ghosts, transparent to crawling darkness. Jacob didn't know when but he'd let go of her hand, and he retook it now. She barely breathed; he grasped her in his arms, dropping the lantern in his haste. Acheronian winds bloomed a million times over. Despite them, he realized, he couldn't see in the dark: out through storms still raging, ectoplasm gathering, metabolics digesting the excess, until finally that roaring turned to waves.

Tinctured singing in a garden of flowers, asphyxiated queens and green chlorophyll growing; she spun (without moving, a meditative togetherness) as does the sky in falling, arms wide above her, closed eyes seeing straight through them. Sunlight fell on bare arms, softgold as day renewed vision; singled embers of feathered chambers, soul bearing to clouds, no weight chaining to earth. For miles grew the fields, plural actuating as one, with no hint of rotting.

We believe in three forms of life: humanity and flowers and light. Light acts as a kind of meta-presence, giving depth of color and fullness of standing, so we might strive higher, and catch more, dispersing proponent nourishment through and because of. To an extent, all are photosynthetic. We grow healthily and easily, like the garden itself.

Laura dreamed of being born into light: weightless opening into an invisible bubble. Nature flowed with presence, particles rising from all that lives. All things move onward, upward, strings of no perceptible width in maintenance of that invisible connection. Hers was strongest of all.

Jacob was coming towards her; he had no eyes, she couldn't see them. She'd nearly lost consciousness the night before, but recalled his talk of visions (plasma fire, nebulous rushing). There could be no memory. She envisioned his face in full color—certainly impossible.

"My father caught me last night," Jacob said, "when I got home." He shifted. "He told me I shouldn't go again, and after that he beat me."

"How did it happen?"

"I arrived home after morning, so he did it outside, in case the Sun God had seen."

"There was nothing to find," she said. "We shouldn't have gone at all."

"How much do you remember?" When she shook her head, he continued: "Before we left there was someone else there too, who looked like you. I saw right before I dropped the lamp. When it went out she was gone."

"I don't do well at night."

"I didn't know."

"You did," she said. "A long time ago, you forgot."

:::::::::::::::::

Walking through the garden, nameless scents combining, she came upon the dead bent stalk of a flower: partially relieved of petals—in haste, it seemed—with damage to the buds. Clear fluid seeped from many wounds, half its length buried in the ground.

To kill flowers was forbidden. In legends there were even tales of divine punishment: a manifestation of the Sun God himself, or some highest messenger, who never spoke, and came with skin of pure fire.

She lifted the flower, making it her companion. A stem by this point, excepting only the lingering threads of petals, she would return these to it, as well as life. Somewhere—as of yet she didn't know where—she would give it an altar.

In one of these places (not the one she chose), she found Gidian. He strummed silently at his instrument, but she saw his fingers move. Subtle harmony collected around him. Blond hair fell past his shoulders, the feminine blond hair he'd always been proud of. Beside him grew three lean trees, their branches sculpting untouchable shapes on him.

It seemed she startled him.

"Sarah?" At her incredulity, he shook his head. "Sorry." He ceased looking at her. "I thought you were someone else."

"You were waiting for someone?"

"No."

"I could leave if you want." She took a step away. "I do need to plant a flower."

"I'm not sure if you know," obviously she did, "but it seems to be dead. Flowers die when you pick them."

"You looked like you were having fun." But really, he looked exactly like he normally did. And he never had any fun. "I'll leave you alone."

"Stay if you like." Though he sighed, a disappointed sound.

She left.

::::::::::::::::::

She overlooked her home from a hill above it. Many rooms were left open to the sky, and these she made out in minute detail. Familiarity had nothing in common with newness.

Someone knocked on her door as she was preparing a meal. Jacob had yet to change his clothes. For moment she wondered why he'd come—having no place here, and no reason to be—but only for a moment. She considered letting him in. She didn't want him here but he deserved that at least.

::::::::::::::::::

New dawn broke with an arpeggio, coming alive like fine music. Narrow beams poked holes in the earth, lighting early moisture; smell of sweet morning and ripe buds, aura at the skin of the land. Laura opened her eyes in a pocket of glowing amber. Every morning she woke earlier than anyone else, just as she had no place in the village at night.

She walked to the window, accidentally taking a sheet with her. Outside spread the dipping gardens, slights and slopes, iridescent. Nothing moved in the rooms below, so her parents hadn't come home yet, and Michelle was certainly still asleep. Gentle warmth settled about her: renewal. She hated the darkness.

For everyone but Jacob, the night was its own species of void, foreign as a long life in a single moment. Even flowers closed, staying that way until the next morning; but now groped openward, organic explosion in pulsing green tubes. In the center of every villager was a clear piece of crystal, with linkages to the arms, the legs, the head and shoulders. When the sun shone, making the crystal shine, everyone began to breath, they were capable of movement again...

Dressing quickly, she went outside. Sabers lanced turquoise wafers, jutting in thin jagged panels, the tight hot sun above them. As always no wind blew. With the exception of two others, no one else had ever *felt* wind. Still drowsy, she set down one of three pathways. Voluptuous forests sprang upon her.

Almost without noticing, she encountered someone in the center of the path—at exact odds with the flower she'd found yesterday, he was neither pretty nor capable of love. She poked him. His eyes opened slowly, as if in pain. A pink bar tore the left side of his face, which he'd slept on, and fine specks stuck to his clothing.

"Oh," he said. "Hello." He looked around. "I didn't make it home."

"Will your father be angry?'

He made a sound something between a sigh a yawn. "Hopefully not. I'll carry a big stick."

"Why did you go home this way?" This path didn't lead to his house. In fact it didn't lead anywhere.

"I went back to get the lamp." Jacob pointed to the grass a few feet away. It looked much smaller when not acting as a mode of consciousness. "And I came out somewhere different. It was really late by then. I wanted to go home, but I fell, and I couldn't get up."

"Did you go to the cave again?"

"It's been there every night for days."

"And you found it in the dark?"

"I brought a candle." That apparently he'd discarded. "But it wasn't the same. I brought this too." He pulled something out of his pocket. A knife. Laura took a few steps back. Then she took another. "I found it in the wall," he said, "next to the picture."

"Why did you take it?"

"It seemed like a good idea at the time."

"What if someone found you?"

"I wasn't holding it out, I just had it in my pocket." He returned it there and came to his feet, dusting himself, but not well.

"Are you—"

"I'm okay." He shook his head. "Just tired."

"Are you going home?"

"Probably not."

"Then walk with me."

He did. He was no good at it. Waking could be painful, as they both knew: torn from a deep hole into which you've molded like plastic, gummy frame to whatever hollow walls. New life pulls the soul through dimensions of distortion, probing with hot irons, hitting with solid objects; a cruel play of internal energies, nefariously squirming. Most frowned upon rousing another from sleep unless it… mattered (something she'd entirely forgotten, at the shock of almost stepping on him), even if she didn't much regret it.

"When we get to the hill today," she said, "you should tell a story."

"What?"

"Well, we all have something we do—Gidian plays music, and I make things grow—but normally you just watch us. You're like an empty space."

"What would I talk about?"

"Tell us about your dream," she said. "Remember something."

They came to the stream, sipping mosses and rock. By its bank lay soft damp sand. The clear surface cast clones of them both.

Two rivers came into the village, crossing and recrossing on occasion, but while one bound itself to the earth, flowing in from over the wall, the other ran suspended in air, washing over trees, grass, and flowers, a hanging curtain of liquid, refracting amidst an aqueous center of mirrors.

They stood now at the first. It was not a long way across. In some places it grew deeper or longer, but from this point they could cross easily. The opposite bank looked much like this, but bore fewer stones, and peculiarly sharp shrubbery. No footprints on either side. Way, way down, the stream swept upwards, on a path to the sky.

"Why would anyone want to climb the walls?" Laura asked.

"No one tries anymore," Jacob said. "It only happens once a lifetime, and when they fail, it becomes a story, and no one tries again until everyone's forgotten them."

"Everyone knows that," Laura said, "except, knowing, they still try."

"I guess that means it isn't true," Jacob replied. "They climb if they have a reason to climb, because they don't want to be here anymore."

"Do you remember?"

"I remember."

"It wasn't that long ago."

"I know."

"Then why did you try?"

"I don't know." And when she asked again, he said—"I was young."

"Did you really want to leave?"

"No."

"Then why?"

Laura realized her anger. She fed on pounding water.

"I have dreams about it sometimes," Jacob said, "but I still don't remember. My father slapped me afterwards." He picked up a rock; tossed it. "I never tried again. I'll never try again. Really."

"This is our home," she said.

"I know that."

"Only madmen leave home."

"I know that too."

They walked across the stream.

:::::::::::::::::::

Something white takes a breath in the flower; nutrient paste races through the roots, panorama of many colors, lifted by working currents. In each is a soul, some shape or form of a soul—pure energy, pure sunlight—that filters such flowing; limbless, internal reflection of body. Mechanical jaws crush in the dirt, full blossom surrounds delicate living core. The energy they create is filtered to the sun, reborn as something not seen but felt. And when the flower dies, the soul rises like holy smoke....

::::::::::::::::::::

"Like words?" Jacob asked.

"I'm not sure. No."

"Just sound, then?"

"They're not talking," she said. "It's a song." The rivers and the trees, subtle symmetry, that dipping hum the wild wild wave; diptych extension, manifold brace, duplicated in sense, nature and miniaturized gods... to roll all day in soft grasses, pillowed as they make way for the body; cast no shadow, greatness to banish all shadows; spacious as wavelengths; rhythm in movement; energy to surge all at once. "The sky sings. The flowers sing. The rumbling earth remembers them."

"But why can't I hear?"

"Maybe you can." She couldn't imagine *not* hearing: the song had become a part of her, like the sun, like the walls, except more, because it felt like she was part of it too. "Just listen." Though no matter how close, he could never. All his world shook with the walls: churn grinding, morph fuse reactions, blood. And really they stood in different worlds—the hateful and the beautiful, the changing and the sane.

Past them wove the high floating river, flooding spirals in the noon.

Gidian's parents were the village elders despite the fact that neither were very old, or possessed much elderly wisdom. Elders just needed to be nice enough, or know how to smile. Preferably both at the same time, if they were overachievers. Not that Gidian called them stupid; most often they spoke for themselves. The village never disagreed about anything, so mostly his parents' duties involved routine meetings. Very often people forgot them, his parents included.

Gidian's childhood was a phantom train of these meetings, bored amongst too many jovial voices, backslapping, reminiscences and halfhearted attempts to pretend the occasion mattered, during which they might plan a few gatherings, and pass large amounts of gossip. We're a small village. Such establishments are necessary to maintain else the difficult times come around. We just hadn't any for a very long time.

Gidian had hair the color of the sun; slender androgynous limbs; smooth pale skin. His mother's friends, until he learned how to scowl, had been fond of pinching his cheek and proclaiming him the most adorable boy they'd ever seen. More recently he'd been catching the attention of their daughters. More recently still, he'd grown fond of large hats.

And he played music.

We all knew his talent, but he refused to play for anyone but himself. Occasionally children lay, uncomfortable, in the fronds behind his secrets spots to listen, and on very rare occasions, based on degree of said discomfort, he let them live. Invariably the melancholy left him, the somber sense of artistry, and his fingers shook, he missed notes—not that they noticed. This went on until such a time as his aim became too precise for others to take the risk.

In the youth before youth, his parents had wanted him to play at meetings (it made them look good), and the only thing he despised more than the meetings themselves was playing at them; so much that at first he hadn't been able to recognize—prostrate in an oddly lit room, instrument in one hand, ball of fire in the other—his anger for the very *intensity* of its sensation. And of course he played horribly, but either they loved him, had no idea what they listened to, or were far, far nicer than anyone could possibly be (he opted for the second), so when he was done they clapped, proclaimed him a prodigy, and ruffled his hair. The last he found most disturbing of all.

It happened five times.

He'd had to break a chair to get out of the sixth.

But it wasn't the villagers' fault, not really. He did like them in his way, much as could be expected. Nor was it selfishness, in the traditional sense. He *couldn't* play around other people because that part of him didn't, couldn't *ever* belong to them.

In many ways, Gidian wondered if he was even human: the center in him. He had the power to create life, to recreate thinking. Alone, he became a focal point of the universe. The leaves lifted, grass fell on its side. Minute fibers made visible, colors like some gleaming web, fiber carbon traces panoramic discourse. Something slipped through in thin channeled streams.

It was a slow process: slower than growing. To intentionally create. The body, a compound of cells and genetic fibers, multiplies not as one but a billion, all at their own function, as dots in a world of dots; but he worked one at a time, simultaneously sustaining, rearranging; and sometimes his world became a gallery of bright colors, shaped like the world but still of it, seeing in it, feeling in it.

Gidian did realize he was selfish, belonging to only himself. Never at any point in his life would he voluntarily attend a legislative meeting, and nor would he devote himself to long walks and the appreciation of beauty. He liked to sulk. No one else knew what that meant, but that just signaled it was working.

And, as has already been mentioned, he had a fondness for large hats—of wide brim and elegant curve, great curvatures in the sun. He had the largest collection in the village (three), and spent much time whispering to them, taking care of them, even occasionally wearing them. One was of soft brown, trimmer and leaner (obviously his least favorite for its comparative lack of girth, even if it did have a certain petty appeal); while the second, also brown, was longer, thinner, and flappy.

The third, his favorite of all, combined the strengths of the two. It was wide, but not so wide it wobbled; tall, but not so tall he knocked it against trees. In color it was dark red, perhaps burgundy, and so gentle he might, if he desired, pet it. He wore it almost every day. Neither timid nor excessively flamboyant, it seemed tailored to him, his counterpart in destiny, predating time—if time before his hat could be said to have a meaning at all....

Gidian wasn't sure where he'd discovered such passion for eccentric headdress. Tales spoke of minstrels dressed this way (breaches and tunic, wide sunbearing brim), but he played for himself, while minstrels played for the people. But it could very possibly *be* the hat one of one such minstrel, as it was apparently quite old, and had something about it of music. He'd asked Laura once if she thought it suited him, and she'd replied (though with a notable lack of enthusiasm, as though she wanted to be somewhere else, or sneeze) that she found it... charming.

His hat had been passed down through the ages, similar to Jacob's lamp, some of Laura's dolls, and even many clothes, despite frequent resewing. The past had its own frequency of vibration: moving slower, tired by that wicked gravity, size and shape in eternal present. Artifacts rarely rusted, always retaining their function, and there were actually storehouses—ignored for the most part, on the assumption of previous excavation—packed into forgotten places, where one might search if they had the will to brave ancient dust. Mostly they were junk, bits of odd metals, broken toys. If there'd been an instrument so beautiful as his it surely would have been gone a long time ago, for it's elegant construction—if not to be played, then at least as a decorative piece, or even a sacrifice. It certainly wouldn't be so well fit to him, sitting perfectly as he held it, playing so clearly when he strummed.

Gidian had discovered the instrument in dreams (so long ago he could barely count, at least a thousand days, two thousand, time beyond what we measure in the valley, where life is life, a day is a day, and everything is either past or future, as we sit isolated in the present, sure of the three [past, present, future] to be maintaining that precarious balance). Many nights he dreamed of it, and the hunger grew like so many monsters, tongued and teethed as his own. In dreams he carved it from the finest base, giving it strings, and woke with it holographed in him, way down in that clear piece of crystal. He treated it like the finest of all hats, with love. It was more beautiful than a woman, than the firmament, and when it sang, it created life.

Like this he carried it for days; later realized that in a sense he'd carried it all the time. Already the children had heard him play, as he sat alone. (Below a tree, next to the stream, it didn't matter.) And in possessing it he became a new creature, not living in the real world like everyone else, where the sun rose each day, and wild rivers cut across the land, and the too familiar walls were always different. And then, without knowing it, he'd been forced to play in front of the village, and he became skilled at throwing rocks.

Each day he waited to go to the hill. The energy felt strongest there, the closer he got to the sun. But it was a scary place later in the day, without the others. It reminded him that the hill was ritual, not a part of his own life. In all truth Gidian thought it somewhat perverse, if not frightening. The closer one got to the sun the less *one* one was, half of two, the possession.

Gidian had gone there only once later in the day, and he'd never gone back. It was a scary place, all shadow, of cold, cold winds. Chilling fingers pried him open; frozen grass attended to welkin gods. Playing music had been like attacking a rock wall, or breathing water. His clothes hung too large—either that or he was getting smaller. The sun shone darkness. Any second it might fall on his stranger self, the intruder.

The temple stood in a clearing in the center of the village, a stretch of empty land around it. Blocks of stone served as a semblance of entrance, and ivy grew on those. From inside the village disappeared. You saw the same hills, identical formations in the land, but where there ought to be houses were plains, and even the gardens differed.

There was no point of transition between these two versions of the valley, or at least none he could recognize. Tradition forbade looking backwards as you passed, and he'd only once found the will to try, at which time Laura had stopped him. There was no barrier he could detect, but from inside it was always the same fields. Just the same was it forbidden to wander these. They'd adventured perhaps a little beyond the base, where the grass turned yellow, but never with the courage to go out further, always struck by the fear of another line, and if they crossed it they'd never come back....

Rarely did two generations of the same family participate in the ritual. He'd spoken to elderly members of the village who invented stories of their frolics there, lying whether they knew it or not, Gidian could tell, the things they told him held nothing of the place he knew. And when he looked closely, they were barely alive. Participants were chosen when they were very young, but their time always ran out. Everyone felt when it was time, just as they felt who should be next—a thought had by everyone at once, made without thinking.

Occasionally Gidian liked to walk along the walls. It was ironic he still called them that, because of course there was only one wall, even if it tended to the plural. Most probably they went back for miles, meaning if there was anything out there, the valley was a *hole* in the earth. It was difficult to conceive of this: sense of vertigo against heavy drowning. Thought of other valleys was ridiculous, the thought of them being populated even more ridiculous. Gidian never went far into the wastelands (named to mean, literally, the wastes at the edge of the world), but liked trailing his boots in them, kicking stones. Like the rest of us he could never really bring himself to be interested in the wall for being so familiar, but such a short distance away, a much further distance up, lie the unexplored world, the inconceivable.

Gidian had never been sure what to call his instrument, nor how to describe it. It was wide, and spread with strings, and made of dark shiny wood, and fit in his hands when he held it. It bore nine strings, some of them different lengths. He played with both hands. If he held down a string, he could hold out notes; running his hand across them, they vibrated softly. Held at certain angles, it looked something like a weapon. Occasionally he sang aloud. Words held their own form of music. Tone, pitch, timbre, rhythm and other qualities he was unable to describe.

He was not the only musician in the village. But he was by far the best.

No. The wraiths that aren't. He didn't and he couldn't.

The wall lurched in its ultimate magnitude; it seemed larger than the world, to consume its entirety. Spilling guts and an avalanche of energy: white cracks stabbed diagonal, miasma surface shifting, whole lakes of billowing gas. Radiance skimmed the outline. Solidity became his field of vision.

The wastes tapered to a slim rim. In their place a mountain rose, splitting to an outline—jagged crystal, crumbling sands, pirouette segments, a wheel. He had no need for footholds, handhold, or anything so menial.

Nothing could stop him. He could not be touched.

::::::::::::::::::::

Dreams of aching fire, wyvern messengers, penultimate green. Wicked lightning turned him into a lighthouse; acid devoured his bones. Hydrochloride thunderclaps: billowing hurricanes. Regenerative phantoms played tricks on direction.

Jacob didn't wake from dreams. He came out of his dark place.

Each day it got harder and harder.

In his dark cold room he shifted, foot against blanket, searching for windows. Bedpost there and thin blankets, he turned in them, blinking once to orient himself, blinking again when it was still dark. The frames and thorns he found; the tails and machines.

But no, he was still asleep.

(engravings...)

He was still asleep.

:::::::::::::::::::

Jacob's father was the only priest in the village. He kept many secrets. Mythology is the closest thing we know to theology, and he the closest thing to a theologian. If he proclaimed the world fire then it was fire, water or air, as it was many things (peninsula upon a stone golem's belly, flicker of impersonal awareness, a single soul), even if we couldn't see, because we didn't have eyes like his, or they weren't open.

The priest may reveal whatever he wished, at whatever time. His library was vast and contradictory, but absolutely devoid of interest. The knowledge must be passed on, but only to one person, that it may still *be* without consequence. When he died (and he would die soon), this replacement would have nothing of the storyteller in him, nor the scholar, nor, especially, the priest.

Jacob would never climb. Not if he had a choice.

:::::::::::::::::::

Nothing painted in an empty room. The chair was flat: the table, the vase, the few flowers. It had a flat door, and the ground was flat; the ceiling too. Fluctuating fire coiled in the walls beyond. It moved.

Vapid shapes: all of them the same. In dreams they came wild and sketched of wire. An abstract sense of construction. It fell apart.

Bronzed statues and glazed iron. New dawn the helix string.

If given a choice, he would never climb the walls.

:::::::::::::::::::

Jacob's father favored silent communication, however ineffective. They rarely ate together. Their house was dark, and dank, and too frightening for visitors. The library smelled like paper. It had nothing of the symbolic in it, a place where words weren't; where they were distant as stars.

Jacob grew up covered in invisible hooks: one, two, three of them, all lifting to some distant anarchist universe, a vacuole darkness lurking somewhere past reason; tinge of unsteadiness, legs like a thorny tree, jerkily swimming the amniotic sea, umbra tinged amber. As a son, from whatever lowly vantage, he witnessed the ultimate unhappiness that bore him—creased lines an on unsmiling face, a commitment to ritual—and had no wish to become it.

Unspoken between them was the need to keep legends secrets. In his life he'd taken many steps, but he never knew where they took him, especially this one. The Sun God did have a name, just as he had many names, and many shapes; just as there were many gods, and many monstrous kinds of people. Being nameless gave him power by making him invisible, just as the past is powerful for being unknowable, and the walls are powerful for being untouchable.

Jacob did not want to be a priest of the Sun God. He had little love for the invisible.

But there was much fear in him of the incendiary, a second person, whom he'd be when he cast off his mortal shell—or when it threw him out. There was nothing inside that flaking skin; nothing in the whole forsaken universe but the invisible, plentiful as darkness.

All life is culminated process: thought, the operation of the body, sight and sense, movement, rushing walls, flowers tangled in growing, grains interlacing in wood, granules of sand, the process of process, movement between movement. Inside him the world was invisible, like a flat painting on a flat wall. No wind reached him. He couldn't even remember who he *was*....

A sliver in a universe of slivers. He didn't have a body because he didn't understand the body; didn't have a world because his god called phantom. And at night he left himself behind, a syncopated absorption: red eyes, no appreciation for beauty. It ate flowers, sinewy muscle in the holographic invisible. He couldn't think without trailing off; couldn't look without seeing another. Old clothes meant little: a fall to noncorpum sentience, will to jump from body, to body, to body... inhuman, he didn't know, the monster in him, there dwelled a monster, skin made of grass, its eyes like globes of clouded quartz.... He dreamed descents through fibrous nocturne galaxies, penumbra scale in the sodium gratings... the universe as seen within a black hole, suffering distension. Whatever traitorous form of darkness.

And the Godhand came to him, saying: Take me now as your own, you who are different, who are the spawn of proliferating Nothing. I am gold and you are crinkled flesh, fermented bones a home to me. The inhuman is in you—the grand, great and displayable—and your soul is made of sticks, stones, and just a few pieces of parchment.

:::::::::::::::::

He always thought he shouldn't come back, but he went regardless.

The cave had appeared on a different side of the village, perhaps the opposite. Starbursts flickered backwards, polyglot tangles above and below. Wicked beams jutted over and across, extending sharp edges to keep him out, to keep him here; the hived vein behind him, the stillness beyond. Frequently he stumbled, and hit his head. Blades of earth invaded him.

Just as he remembered: a flat room. Statuary collections, pottery displays, shelves full of many strange objects; he walked among them, between them, bringing illumination and life... this two dimensional museum, hearthstone to coplanar glories; he touched them and felt nothing, felt everything more. In the village artists took things and created another of them, duplicating hills, bifurcating flatness. There, everything had a counterpart that made them real already, but was that true here as well?

Jacob pressed against the wall. To be thin and papery tissue, to be here without moving. He elongated, taking on the properties of pastel, height and shape, like a painting on flatness, his ink still shining, nose and lips in suspension, his eternal clothes. To be part of the mirror; some living.

He reflected himself without counterpart on the outside, carving something finely hewed with fingers of stone....

::::::::::::::::::

Aether tendrils reached out for him, their inky ribbons unfurling: the claws of a many eyed demon, dweller of the curled space. He lived in a toy box of silence, where the serpents crawled. Wildfire sprang from the evening, and everywhere were whirling trees. Bitterness on his tongue. Reliving.

He woke much later, maelstrom energy, electron racing whatever nuclei semblance. He stood in darkness. Stalactite lurching obstacles; he pulsed. New life set him stumbling, really nothing in that intravenous tubing. Unbearable hunger and he was strengthless, breathless, without a body. Ghost-currents swept from way back, lifting onto clouds, carrying him forward.

He fell: gasp and choke.

Past his eyes (he had none), bent stalks received him, lurid beds abounding. There he slept without sleeping: a real and terminal sense of falling, into whatever void the soul braces, where nothing moves, and not even the universe breathes....

Instead it was the hazardous rise, above himself onto gray hazes, phantasmagoria of souls... white, white lights, a million at once, swimming a dull clouded sky, full mists and regenerative body... laterally transmigrating, blazing in energy... and a song issued from them, invisible wind through petals, grandiose as the flailing sun, symphonic resounding in the sky....

From his body he rose... he rose, and rose, and rose, and no chains held to the skin, nothing in the valve of his heart, no burrow in that clear piece of crystal.

And then he fell.

Down, and down, and down, but slowly, a floating soul, a detached, impersonal form of a soul....

::::::::::::::::::

He woke, sun in his face, deadly weight in him. Pulling to his feet was difficult. He fell into shade. Disbanded, the wanderer. He wandered until some girl found him. Golden hair fell around her face, and she wore a soft white dress.

He didn't realize for many sentences that he knew her—that as she spoke to him, he ought to say something in return. Her name was something like Lauren. It was something.

"It's okay," he said. "I'm fine, really."

"You've been gone for two days," she said.

"I'm fine."

"You've been—"

"I'm fine."

As he spoke reality broke, tessellating parallelograms in being, strange lines on straight shapes, paragon dusting to the nth degree, devout following, falling, his distended semblance, a whirlwind twirling, gaping cup, outstretched fingers, overmatched, that every night he might sink into deserts of feathered skin, buried comfortably in a market of corpses. The caricatures stood with him, the vultures and the swine, and they made carrion modifications: beak, hood and feathers, clawed hands, an inspired sense of fighting. Explosions rang out over gaps in space, in time, and he sank. Drifts of glass.

He sank.

Sunshine in the Valley

Whenever Laura asked if someone had seen Jacob—an old woman standing by her home, two children by the river, a father tending his garden—invariably the answer would be no. Jacob exuded invisibility.

Wide ringlets spread to either side, noontime vines and the heavy light of day. Did she miss Jacob? She pretended to sometimes, but she didn't like him very much. He was always too impulsive, rambunctious, and stupid. But she couldn't feel him anymore, and he left a Jacob sized hole, contoured to his still growing chest, old clothes, scarcity of definition.

Did she run? Where, and why, but it certainly felt she did. Running had never been easy for her, involving such variables as the need to lift her dress, to step carefully, to breathe. Wherever she was going.

She found Gidian somewhere else. He always looked the same, like half a person, sitting below trees, sunlight glowing off that ridiculous hat. He had a fondness for dressing all in one color, like a splotch of paint on background.

He looked far, far too happy to see her.

"Have you seen Jacob?" she asked

That happiness went away.

He hadn't.

Leaves fell between them, around them, above them; pieces of the tree already dead or dying. Gidian looked like the melodramatic *idea* of a person, one who had very little idea what it meant to be human.

"Who were you waiting for?"

"No one."

"But I could tell," she insisted, "there was this look in your eyes like you—"

"—Enjoy being sneaked up on by beautiful girls." He shrugged.

At which point he began to ignore her.

Having a conversation with Gidian could be the strangest thing. You didn't notice, but while you were talking he never stopped playing, actually looking past you, looking *through* you, like clear glass into whatever basin he thought you a shadow.

::::::::::::::::::::

Laura laid a blanket in the grass. Michelle probably should have helped, but, like always, she confined herself to useless and idle standing. Their parents had gotten home earlier that morning, but they hadn't come, so they weren't helping either. The basket Michelle carried (at least she was good for *something*) held delicious things, the edible kind. Despite multiple attempts, the blanket persisted in its wrinkles.

Michelle looked strangely pretty, wearing a nice dress and a bow in her hair—not that it changed her, because beneath them (though outside herself) she remained the same person. But Laura did have to admit, sometimes, that she was almost glad to have a sister. As long she wasn't talking.

There were only two at the center of the village that day.

"He's never been late before," Laura said. Gidian replied that today Jacob had made an exception. But they were *never* late, and there was no such thing as an exception. "We have to go find him."

"Why?"

"He needs to be here. You know that."

"It's nice like this." He smiled. "We get along."

Laura glared at him. "We never have. You know that too."

"Do you miss him?"

"Yes. Obviously. And if you were a friend, so would you."

But she couldn't tell, *did* she miss him, or was she just using Jacob to fill some abscess in herself—whatever humanity she did have?

(Was it making her tired?)

(Did her life have room for remedial sleep, the kind that didn't involve falling?)

She didn't leave, of course. They had to stay at least the greater noontime, until there came blurs in that thin-edged crescent, folding ever so lithely inward. The remainder of the day she spent exploring the village, wherever. She didn't know what she went for; didn't know if she searched either, or just projected her stationary self, from whatever place, to look in her stead, without finding.

The next morning she visited Jacob's house. His father opened the door slowly, like a predator. He gave her absolutely no help, and shut the before door before she could even say goodbye.

Wherever she went. She didn't know how to look for a missing person in such a small place, even if she told herself she could still find him, because he was still here, wasn't he? By accident she visited the same places as yesterday, perhaps in exactly the same order.

She found Gidian again, despite his stealthy reputation, and had absolutely no wish to speak to him.

She chose not to.

The valley was not a world of trees. Most were rather thin, with trunks you could wrap your hands around, forcing her to wonder if there had been more a long time ago, before the invention of houses. Taller trees had an impossible number of names carved into them. She sat beneath one, its energy behind her, its closeness reassuring.

Soon after standing, she found Jacob. In a manner of speaking. He stumbled down the road as though recently awoken from sleep, just much worse than a person. With each step he staggered, bending at lateral degrees, marionette arms waving, chest quaking, shake-dancing patterns. Unsurprisingly, his eyes held little focus. Laura wasn't sure, but he might have drooled.

"Jacob?"

He looked at her like some estranged variety of ghost, trying in some measure to stand; failing. Had she gotten the name right? *Was there even anything to find?*

"You've been gone for two days," she said. He squinted, tilting his head.

"I'm fine," he said. Obviously.

She shook her head. "I don't think you understand," she said, "you've been gone—" Whereat he waved a dismissive hand, repeated badly considered observations of his condition, and promptly collapsed, one boot shooting into the air. The whole motion had something of a "wriggle" in it. Boneless. Laura wasn't sure if she should scream, help him up, or drag him.

As it happened she was too busy covering her mouth to accomplish the first, unable to wake him, and not nearly strong enough to drag—she did try, at least, and got perhaps five or six steps before dropping him. At this point she ran back to the village, not quite screaming for help but asking with vigor, whereupon a handful of villagers, half of whom knew nothing of the disappearance, none of whom had helped her before, carried Jacob to his father's house.

Much as Jacob had explained (she'd never been inside), it was a scary place, where the light couldn't get. Floorboards creaked, and corners didn't make any sense. It had a broken chandelier. Shelves bathed in dust and refuse, as though no one had lived here for a million days, as though no one had *ever* lived here.

The priest opened the door. He moved to cane her before seeing his son at her feet. (She stood alone by this point, as when they'd gotten near the house all the villagers had run away, leaving her to drag it the last twenty steps or so.) It had gotten late; she had little idea how. Cool evening lashed the ceiling, and shadows coerced in darkness. Light, or its nighttime pretender, thrust past slats, staining dull framework. Outside, it had turned the old man's face to a gothic caricature, ample decor on hideous fundament.

Not far away lay Jacob, or his shell, not moving, one arm crossing his chest, the other hanging in air. Bringing him inside, cloak ballooning as he spun, the priest had laid him on a table (she struggled in thinking of him as Jacob's father, now more than ever), chanted, and stood almost furiously, baring his purplish crescent of a frown, until, like a gas, he floated into another room.

Laura wasn't sure where she was supposed to be, but she hadn't been told to leave. She wasn't sure but probably she felt responsible, though more and more she didn't know what she felt. Emotions were such a tumultuous game, and she'd never been inclined to differentiate—finding herself now in the answerless, questions about herself second only to questions about everything else. She wished Jacob would move. Where was he? Had she even brought him back?

But she realized belatedly that he did move, breathing as he slept. She noticed her own rapid breathing, wondering why she hadn't noticed it before.

First she thought to scream, but having never been inclined to such, she refrained; refrained also from telling Jacob's father. She was too scared to go near him, just as, at the moment, she feared Jacob himself. So she stood for many minutes, until the sun fell completely; became tired herself, and fell past the dirty floor.

She woke next morning at first glint, leaning painfully against the wall, pale light shining in the gloom wherever. An ache lanced her neck; dress dirty from the floor. Disorientation wailed at her—*where are you where are you where are you*—until she remembered to think, and stood. Closed shutters, empty cupboards, did not make for a glorious reawakening.

She thought little of the empty table—it being, for all practical purposes, just a gross, rather unpleasant looking table—until she realized that by extension it meant Jacob was gone. She looked for his father also, but found only his shadow.

Outside, recurrence struck at her, the feeling of having done this before; also the feeling of coming *unstuck in time*, as though something she'd done, some transition (finding Jacob, opening the door, sleeping) were enough to dislocate her from the temporal universe, misdirecting currents onto whole unfamiliar realms of passage. She asked the same question, got the same answer, and nobody (nobody!) volunteered to help.

The next morning, before she woke, she could have sworn she saw a girl standing above her bed, short hair and pale face, dim polished by morning, but it must have been a dream.

Laura needed to quit sneaking up on him like this. Gidian feared her invisibility. This idleness of his had gone past measurement, to become a lateral dispersion of the soul.

"Oh," he said. "It's you."

"I need your help."

"Go away."

She asked why not. He said he didn't care: he had better things to do, and he liked to make her angry. Gidian supposed he'd always thought that, about most every girl he knew. Her fury radiated energy like a star—not that an angry girl had much cosmic about her, other than danger of vast explosion, and by extension, incinerating death. And he didn't appreciate being sneaked up on again… *he thought* it was three times, but she might be keeping a record, just because she didn't like him; he had more than one body, so he could never tell.

"You *have* to help," she said. "I spent two days looking for him—alone, I might add—and now, as soon as I've found him, he's gone again."

Gidian didn't remember ever hearing her yell like this, or even raise her voice.

Apparently she was full of surprises.

He told her no again, and felt satisfied. But then she was almost crying, and if he said no everything would change, because of what she'd put at stake. If not herself than everything else. He wasn't sure what she wanted, but he had the power to cut strings, a crisis of one and one equaling one, equaling none.

He was no golem. Nor did he carry a pair of scissors.

"Okay," he said, "but I need to finish something, so wait just a while." It might be more, but he would go. He hadn't expected any gratitude this late (except perhaps a smile, that also he didn't get) but she left cords in place, instead of her own un-presence; and he felt, somewhere inside, as though he'd saved at least a passably significant area of the universe.

Half that while later (maybe less, he congratulated himself, feeling for once like a good person, despite not caring for the sensation), he stood, shook his hat, and had no idea how one went about finding runaway Jacobs. If Laura were around he'd be able to ask her, but then he'd have to look for *her* too, and he was in no mood for paradox.

He settled for wandering.

If one could know the valley, changing as it did, he knew it better than anyone but maybe Jacob (another paradox... or maybe it was irony, he didn't care), even taking into consideration his considerable ego, and tendency to exaggeration.

That ought to help.

During this journey he found only one person—neither of the people he needed. He hadn't realized it, this being in many senses a subconscious phenomenon, but he'd begun to play a song, maybe he'd call it his "Wanderer's Ballad", that quite brilliantly captured the dimensions of his journey: lazy marching, sense of purposelessness, dullness. He congratulated himself on his dexterity if nothing else, and found a clearing so similar to the one he'd come from it might have been the *same* clearing (and maybe it was), to work on it more, in silence.

He played until it seemed he fell: vibrant aura and one gratuitous harmony, sinking, or spreading, until consciousness fanned outwards, awareness percolating dimension, heavenwide confirmation of presence. Whole lifelines glowed and he struck; or the virility didn't leave him. Beams of light spun in the sky—spectral slides in vacant firmament, illumine rides dividing—and an elemental compression built up in him, not just fire, but earth and water and wind, verve and fullness and completion; vigorous freefalls of energy, vitality, music. Whirlwind spins in gravitation. Earthquakes. Gidian didn't know what came to him, what came through, but he flew; borne by interminable currents, resplendent within polyglot energies, whatever transcendence; and he had a vision of the valley as seen from the bottom of a well—it *was* a well, dark aqueous bricks, brightness fulminating past, sight wild-rushing through one momentous tunnel, so large it wasn't a tunnel anymore but the entire world, a fountain....

Soon he woke back in that shell of him—but it was still very handsome, he thought, for being skin. Evening birthed into an early stage of darkness. Slants duplicated shadows. His skin imagined wind, but if it had been a person (separate, that is), he might scold it for being unreasonable. He sat uncomfortably. Someone made a sound.

"Laura?" But she shook her head, and immediately he knew. He shifted, and actually set his instrument on the ground. Grass in the silent, invisible wind.

"I knew you'd come," he said. "I waited for you earlier."

He stood, walking towards her.

"Are you going to talk today?' He took another step, and took off his hat too, so she could see his beautiful hair. "I'll wait as long as you want, and I'll always be ready to listen."

But even though she wanted to, she didn't say a word.

::::::::::::::::::::

Interesting how delicate can be wayward thoughts, how ominously they bludgeon. We all have a monster, however deeply buried, and at times it shows its head, spitting fumes, rubbing its tusks, hunting; we who are neither hunter nor hunted, but the quiet repast of imaginary futures, skidding in a millennium dance, never toppling else we lose that one precious edge, rigidity of muscle, skeletal structure, seeing. In all of us there is a monster.

Gidian found Laura, who he wasn't looking for, but they walked together, if nothing else to be double. It made sense, and they went many places, seeing the garden from perspectives within mazes. Neither spoke of it, but inside they'd always thought that if they just searched hard enough, someday they'd stumble into a hidden roadway, signals and signs—up and over, up and over, up and over—but the roadway never came.

Not often did they speak. They weren't going anywhere, or even on a search, but they bounced in many directions. When they found a rock, they knew assuredly that before a rock it was a boulder, or a stone, and you could sit on it but inside it would always be a rock. When they found the stream it was flowing. When they found they were just two people, a boy and a girl, not young not old, on a journey to no place living, nothing refracted in that clear piece of crystal, but the will to forsake understanding, or become monsters, they didn't know what it meant to think anymore.

We are, and have always been monsters. Always somewhere is the want to eat flowers. The walls keep us to ourselves from the extraordinary world, the inhuman. We're a race of monsters; we have a body, breath and skin, eyes legs arms hands breasts pelvic muscle glutamate sweat an underlay of bones—but no trace of a soul, just clear energy the parasite, we are.

After so long not looking they found a clearing, and a quiet place, and they barely remembered. Were they too young, too old, what were they? If you can't remember birth: in a universe where (maybe) nothing can be created or destroyed, just made to hold shape, like clay. What logic do we have? We who are inbred, generation upon generation of inbreeding, fine genderless angels. With gender.

The suspended sun above them, the walls below it, the river above that, the grass underfoot, and they in-between. Our world is projected memory; our universe, at the atomic scale, polarizes extremity. We are the smallest grain in a grainy desert. We are the written memory of our ancestors; multilingual body of a distant god; we are music. No, we are all of these and none, unprovable as they are invisible, fractal scatterings, a loathsome wind. It's not worth pretending the marionette without strings—neither the puppeteer—they cyclone together, peeling layer and layer and layer, until nothing is big enough to hold them, until they encompass themselves, returning. The maze grew dark and green and deep, auricular fronds like ailing fingers. These gardens hold nothing if not invisible.

Purplish ivy crawled the trees. Leaves rotted that fell. This whole village is nothing if not invisible. Wherever they went.

They did find Jacob eventually. Before him, for a great distance, the walls reached inward, forming a path, even a walkway, smooth among crags and stone, framing a gateway. Jacob stumbled awkwardly, the empty thing that stumbled, wearing Jacob like his monster wore him, like it still wore him, invisible. Nearby the path broke upwards. They couldn't see his face, and even if he'd turned, he wouldn't have seen them. The sun had set for hours now: still setting so slowly, without disappearing until so had his silhouette. If he'd had a choice he never would have left the village, but where was he, buried in puppets and strings and monsters? Every few steps he fell, but the walls were there to catch him, pillars with hands, even with faces. As he climbed, stone heads congratulated, making toasts, slapping him on the back. Rock crumbled and retracted, the body of the barrier. From below, wailing, came a man dressed all in black (they recognized him distantly as Jacob's father, if he was), bursting through foliage, both hands extended, grasping for holds, searching for ankles, screaming *Don't leave without me* screaming *Please you can't I'm coming with you* screaming *You can't go you can't you can't you can't you can't* scratching until his fingers bled, getting hold of dust, screaming *You were supposed you were supposed to take me with you...* until finally he really fell, weeping on both knees, blood streaming from where he'd broken his nose, as above him surged whole helix-realms of energy, and tricks in the light made it appear as though Jacob had grown wings.

II

My name is Sarah. Sometimes that's what I call myself.

I live in an abandoned shack near the edge of the village, where nobody goes, except me. It feels like a home, but only some of the time, if I'm there. I can be more places than one, and have five hundred eyes. Most of them are a part of me. I look like a little girl, and I'm barely a hundred days old.

My first memory is of father. I think he *is* me somehow—either that or I'm part of him, or we're the same thing, except not together. I'm sarcastic like he is, but sometimes I'm not, and I like to tell stories, so much I never stop.

The longer I stay the more I doubt myself, who I am, where I'm going. I have trouble telling the difference between myself and trees, but that doesn't seem like such an abnormal problem. I like to think I'm not an abnormal girl, even without living the way other girls do, and breathing. Not that I don't try, it's just I have trouble remembering sometimes, when I have better things to do.

I whisper to myself in my mind, if I have one. I'm not sure that's normal but there's no one to tell me so I have to find out and the only person I can ask is myself. I make good company, and I can be quite charming. Sometimes I flatter myself, at which point I pretend modesty, not that I'm fooled.

The stories I tell come from the only world I know. Maybe I could leave, but maybe I couldn't, and the part of me that does research (she's rather too serious for my taste, as though she weren't just a part of me; meaning another me, meaning myself) always told me I couldn't, because everyone else told me that. Only crazy people climbed the walls, and I didn't want to be crazy.

Sometimes I can see into people minds, so I know what they think, and what they see; and sometimes I find that without being there I know already. I'm not sure if it's impolite. I've asked occasionally, but I still haven't figured out how to make noises. They've never really seen me, except a few times. And father, when he's looking for me.

I'm not sure I have a body yet either. Maybe that means I'm not real, but having taken consensus (so many factors at play, such as my being silent, invisible, and for all appearances a ghost, as opposed to thought, that ought to signify existence—despite my being divided on that also, and debating furiously), all I do is get in arguments with myself. I always win, and always lose. They never seem to go anywhere.

My earliest memories are of father. He's not really my father of course: he's my mother too, and my brother, and I don't have a sister other than myself, but if I did, he would probably be my sister too. He did make me, by doing whatever with himself. I'm not sure I understand because *he* doesn't understand either.

I don't remember anything very well past a certain point. I've only been counting from the time I *could* count, or at least the time I told myself I could count. I remember his face, and the grass, and the wind, and streams of fire from the sky, and weird vibrations all in me and my tummy, like I was a doll he was stitching, or a statue he carved, though I don't like the idea of being a statue, because then he's stabbing me with a pick, and hitting me with hammers, and I think I'm afraid of pain.

He was always so nice to me, even when I wasn't there, and he was never nice to anyone else. Not even the girl that looked exactly like me. He spoke gently, and he played beautiful music. I didn't understand him, especially because he was a blur at first, like everything else, that just swirled, but when the blur went away he was there, and he was so patient, he understood I wasn't quite there yet. He waited.

I realized after a while that he could only see me sometimes, when he tried his hardest. I always do my best to be there, but it's hard. The other day a leaf fell through me, and that doesn't help me win that argument about being real. I do my best not to argue, I'm pretty sure it's not normal, but I'm still learning how to think, so I can't help myself.

When I first came to life I was his perception of myself, so I saw myself through his eyes, and it was the transition from him, to everything, to me. I have a shape (or I will, he told me), but I'm not quite there yet. Maybe someday, when I'm better at thinking, and I stop arguing with myself (he doesn't know, but I asked myself what he would say, and I said he said it would get easier), he'll be able to see me all the time, and I'll be able to make noises.

When I go to the hill with them I laugh and run and play with them, and sometimes I forget I'm not real; and sometimes, when we sit in a circle, they leave a fourth spot for me, whether they know it or not, and I tell stories. I imagine their hands in mine. They laugh, and I'm not sure if they're laughing at my stories but I don't care, maybe they will someday, when they can really see me, when I am.

Sometimes I forget about me. I become a rock, or the stream (looping around myself), or the grass, or a flower. Just not the sun or the walls. They scare me, and there are people in there already: a billion of them, some of them screaming. Or maybe there's just so many they can't possibly say anything, and when they sing everything clashes, because they're hitting every note at once.

I know lots about music from father. He told me I came from music, that I *am* music, in myself, and that I was his favorite song, ever and ever. He's been working on me for many, many days. He said I was beautiful.

She taught us laughter, he said. *She was*
with us in the morning.

That's my song. In fact whenever I'm around he's singing, if only in his mind. I won't really be there until the song's done. But sometimes I wonder if the song's really about me. I'm me, but I look like someone else, so I'm not myself, and I don't have any sort of oneness. Everything comes from something, even nothing, but if you can't separate it from yourself, you're never really there.

I wish I was better with knowledge; that I could agree. My judgments are too rash. I tend to talk about things I don't understand, especially myself, especially when I ask a question.

When I come to father we sit together. Sometimes he holds me, or he does his best, and I can pretend his fingers don't go through my skin. He sings to me and tells me stories, and points to things and describes them, and sometimes I smile (or normally I do, when I can remember. That's what other girls do when they talk to him, they smile), and we stay together until I'm not really there anymore, even when sometimes I am and he just can't see me, and it makes him sad, or it makes me sad and I just can't tell what I'm feeling, so he feels it, and it confuses me and I don't know where to go anymore.

The other day I tried to eat. By myself. I didn't do very well. I'm not sure if I wasn't hungry or I just wasn't trying enough but even when I (barely) managed to get the food off the table (I'm not sure what it was anymore, or even if it was food) a few times I couldn't get it up to my face and when I did (by kneeling next to the table) it just fell right through me and landed with a plop.

It's still there too. And it's gross.

I'm trying to get involved in interior decorating. I can't carry anything yet, and really my house doesn't have much of an interior (the walls are falling apart, there aren't any doors or windows, sun comes in through the ceiling), but if it did, and I had hands, it would be so pretty. I would dress it up so many colors and get great, great furniture. Right now it's just happening in my mind, but that's real enough for me. When I close my eyes (I have to imagine real hard for it to work) I can almost see everything, just the way I want it. But then I get excited, and I open them too soon, and everything's still just the same, and I have to close my eyes again.

I get sad sometimes. I pretend to cry. And sometimes I feel like my soul, if I have one, is about to fall out, like a big heavy ball inside me on a shelf or tied in a rope I don't know about, but if I don't hold on hard enough it's going to fall out, and I won't be here anymore. There aren't any tears, I haven't figured out how to make them yet, but it's the only way I manage to make noise. And that just makes me cry harder, because I don't sound human yet, I just squeak, and make funny choke sounds, and sob, and sob, and whine so hard my imaginary throat feels like its going to come out too, and I'll vomit myself, all breaking out of my phosphorescent universe, that isn't even a body yet.

I'm not sure why I'm so sad. Father said I was a happy song. Maybe it's because I'm so young. If I was a person, or if I was a real one, I wouldn't even know how to talk yet—not that I do—and I wouldn't be able to think, or stand, or understand what it means to be sad (if I do).

I pretend other times than just at the hill. I walk through the village pretending to smell the flowers, and when I walk by someone I'll pretend to wave. And sometimes they'll even look up but they never see me, so all I can do is pretend to walk away, and be sad, and I don't feel like pretending anymore because it's no more real than I am.

Sometimes I feel how many of me there are. I feel much more stable when I'm around myself. When I just think, or argue, or tell stories, I forget I'm me, even who made me, and by pretending to think I get more real. It's just I can't keep it up for long, because it's hard to forget something that's so much a part of you. I just come back, and it gets worse, and all I have is another story to tell. I know lots of things but for some reason I can't make any sense of them. Except when I'm telling stories. The different me's, inside me, can't agree on a singular me. It's getting better slowly, but I've never been connected to the passage of time.

I actually probably know more about the village than anyone else but that doesn't help at all, all it does is take something and make it separate from me. No matter how much I read and how many times I watch I can't understand because I can't process information right. Inside I'm like a thousand village elders, none of whom agree, so I can't escape the chain reaction of me, the mist and the shell.

But people *are* starting to see me. Or I think they are. I followed Jacob into the cave a few times. He saw me each time, and the last time he even starting talking to me like father, though he didn't get the name right.

He almost made me cry from being happy. I felt real, or more real, and right now that's all I can hope for.

He didn't know, but I knew more legends than he did. More than anyone but his father. I've read lots of those books—when I think back I really don't know how I did it, but I don't know how I *do* anything—and I remember them better, even if I can't understand them. They make me sad too, but I can't help reading.

I hoped at first I'd find what it meant to be a person, but instead I find everything else, and I have to piece and piece and do puzzles and put the pieces in a different order and talk to myself for days before anything makes any kind of sense.

The books are made of old, old paper. Jacob's father seems to have read them all. Every once and a while I read over his shoulder, pretending I have to, but it seems like he can see me (or hear me at least, like I'm a wind on the other side of the room, not that he would know what that is), and I don't like being in the same room with him when he can see me because he's a scary scary kind of guy and I don't like that. He has really big eyebrows darker than anything else on his face. He narrows them at me. He makes funny sounds as though he's thinking of going for a weapon. Whatever I am, he thinks I'm a living shadow, or a ghost made of smoke.

Jacob's father is the only person I don't want to see me. It seems like he's the only one who really can. Jacob, whenever I follow him out of the cave, doesn't seem to notice me anymore. But he hasn't been thinking well recently. I think he thought I was his imagination. It was rude of him.

Other people have seen me—Laura too, I think, while she was almost asleep—but it doesn't matter, they don't recognize me as what I am. I have trouble staying in one place at a time, as opposed to being everywhere, in everything, and not myself, but it doesn't matter, even when I *do* I'm not myself. I'm part myself, and I'm part someone else, and sometimes I can't tell which one I am.

Life without Jacob wasn't so different from life *with* Jacob. Laura hardly saw him when he wasn't taking her on secret, inconclusive adventures, and she didn't particularly want to. He had a self-importance complex, and he was barely even there.

He'd been gone three days already, but the villagers just thought he'd run away again. No one believed when she said he'd gone over the wall because no one had *ever* gone over the wall. Other than the ones that had helped her yesterday, she didn't care enough to make his absence known.

Her parents were gone again, but Michelle was awake, if barely. Night had fallen, and firm blackness set about them, a soupy opaque deepness. After making her journey (she'd thrice traveled the distance of the known world) it baffled her coming home to this; and no, she told herself, her house didn't have legs, and nothing would ever happen in it, except that she would live in it, probably for a very long time, until she got married, if she could bring herself to put up with a man.

So would that be her life? Thirty thousand days then a fall into recurrent sleep, from which there was no waking world, and waking paled, an iridescent lie; wondering then that it could hold at all, for how *thin* it felt, this uncomplicated layer, polish of mirrors... if she only looked hard enough, she could *see*—the way dimension peeled backwards, much like the skin of an apple, smooth and bitter, thin and brittle—until that vaginal blackness, her coin and cage, layer beyond layer; until she was in that, and swam in clear pools made of stars....

More than anything she didn't want to take care of her sister. And where were her parents? She didn't want to imagine that rarefied void, yet her whole life they had filled it with nothing. For the first time she wished Jacob were here. She didn't trust anyone else enough (especially not Gidian), but she wanted someone with her, and Jacob had always been good at filling space—a cold body.

Next morning she woke outside with her face in the grass, for whatever reason. She didn't remember coming out here, but she must have. She stood and felt disturbingly unclean. It wasn't like this. She tired.

She discovered an open door. Dust turned the familiar to haze, triumphant glaze about it. Michelle lie sprawled over the sofa, one leg jutting to the side, wearing a mask of her hair, in a heap of tangles. The floor had never made the noise it did today, and she bumped into corners.

She ate and bathed (the second involved leaving the house, so she made the journey twice), and left her sleeping sister to whatever alternate reality. Inside, heat shimmered. Going out didn't make it any better, but now she had somewhere to be. An indeterminate distance back, she'd forgotten her sandals. Every step renewed memory, over the shallows to fill in bits of odd lines; before the long passing day, the nights.

Upon a slope, purple leaves hung before and beside. They filtered riotous screaming, growing as she approached: a familiar voice, bereft of gender, but taken to new dimensions in fury. She had trouble placing it—she wasn't sure, but she didn't think she'd ever heard anyone scream before—until, close enough to make out a semblance of language, she saw Gidian in his manic gesticulation, waving his fists, kicking stones, spitting. The three men before him were very tall, and looked as strong as men can possibly be when they spend their lives tending flowers. One had a dark, shuffling mustache, probably waggling as he spoke, and another the deepest tan Laura had ever seen, like he'd been cooked in a fire. Whenever Gidian lunged they threw him back—so they were tough enough to fight him away, if there'd been any doubt. Still screaming, Gidian reminded Laura of her baby sister when she'd still *been* a baby, as spit trailed from her mouth, crying hard enough to cough entrails. She wondered what he would say if he heard that.

"What's going on?" she asked.

Gidian wasn't in any condition to say, but past his shouting the guards explained that he wasn't to be let inside today—and by extension, neither was she. One by one they apologized, holding Gidian at bay (still clawing, with sharp fingers), but they didn't seem very sorry.

Laura stopped, stuttered, and for all the world couldn't figure out why it felt as though she'd been chopped in half.

It wasn't sadness, exactly (that would come later), but hollowness, digging way back in her stomach, where her soul might be, to accommodate a cancer; and without understanding why, she found herself capturing tears, golden spheres on the periphery of vision, a need to look anywhere but the world... already wondering why it felt she'd left something of herself, the most important part, buried a million miles away where no one would ever go, in a labyrinth clogged by snow, under lakes of acid, in a furnace.

"Oh," she said.

That's why.

"I'm sorry," one repeated. He smiled, showing three uneven teeth, and in a buried place within her, where the evil was, she wished she could take that face and shatter it, voracious burst into cosmic flux of particles, weltered sparkle in tooth jagged bone. Inside she grew empty, some corner, and the sun shined into an empty room, really no spark in that clear piece of crystal.

She wasn't sure where she went. Wherever. She discovered, among other things, that the body has its own mind, a witless trickster of a mind, and also discovered what it meant to be taken over by that other self. She didn't know where she was, but it was a place of mazes, fenced within green walls....

Inside that, she found Gidian—without knowing, by this point, if he might not have found *her*. He was less composed than usual, and his face had a *tiredness* to it. Impotent. This was the first time she hadn't come upon him in the midst of a song. Instead he made patterns by swinging his foot, tiring as he watched a world that didn't move: far stretch into amnesiac evening, aflutter.

She sat beside him. Neither spoke. Of all the people she knew she wanted to see Gidian the least. But she'd never had good luck. Every so often he changed position, but it was a slow, slow creeping, unconscious too, and both of them, they were just fiber and bones, glazed sheets on sterling plaster.

"It was Jacob's fault," Gidian said, "because he ran away."

"Yeah," she said. "I know."

"I think I hate him. For being inconsiderate." He spat. "Jacob was never much good at thinking."

Laura followed the movement of many petals, a blatant cyanide scrambling, pink waves catching fractal mobility. Even flowers took the shape of the sun: the trees, the walls, her own eyes.

Later, then, she came upon a graveyard of flowers: chewed off stems, the dry grasping roots, piled like a tapestry of bones. Standing before it, she couldn't remember ever feeling so lost. No wind came to her. She would never feel wind again: part of her past life, still so heavily balanced—a continent, landmasses and seas. Derelict conundrum, her idea of the beautiful. All her life she'd born a triumphant pair of wings, and she didn't know if she could bear it with nothing to make her stronger.

Sometimes she had weakness in her (she couldn't help thinking of it as a little girl, so familiar she couldn't tell it from herself), and in times like these, the arsenic days, always she moved faster and faster into a corner, a spectator amid roaring, where she wasn't one person but many. There was nothing she could do.

It was late, but she couldn't go home yet, so she wandered: first between trees, giving them new names (as many had done throughout history, weaving a tapestry) then to the river, a cycling ambient multitude, glass-shining towers, persuasive currents an engine. She followed beside it, sometimes below, amidst the angles' evolve. Different patterns went different ways. Both arms she spread, as though she flew, catching wind in weightless feather sails....

She removed her clothes by the bank, ruffled dress in a pile there, and took a step inside, first one hand in the primordial cool, before it drew all over, becoming her.

She opened her eyes whole eons above the ground, still soaring, elongated into a cloudform. The river carried her weightless. She took a breath. Crooked crystal sunlight: diamonds made of rainbows. Precious stones clung all about her, a lifting presence against her belly, forward motion in circuit.

She fell asleep, or must have, and woke next morning—from particle showers, kaleidoscope fragments—in a four sided clearing; dry, but still naked. Bright yellow proclaimed new morning, and snowflakes rose lazily upward. She stood, but she probably wasn't awake enough to stand, so she fell. Already she wished she'd never woken up.

Probably she should go home first, but she thought she had some idea where she might find her dress, so stealthily as she could (not very), she crept, not very far at a time, down the pathways she found, still with only a vague idea of her location. Thus came her introduction to paranoia: quick glances; many, many leaps to either side; a desperate geometric attention to how much of herself she could cover at one time, while walking.

Knowing very rarely did anyone wake early as she, she might have run, but fear of her own nakedness, not to mention she'd just woken into some alien wilderness, overrode that logic—fear especially of her breasts, so new (in this time and waking moment, as opposed to others) she wasn't sure if *she'd* seen them yet.

She saw no one. But neither did she find her dress. And now, very angry (unwilling to think of what ungodly pervert might have taken it), moving at a slightly more reckless pace, ran quickly as she could towards home.

Unsurprisingly, Gidian found her. Or she found him. Either way. And she discovered how unfair the geometry really was. Despite herself, she felt extremely, unbelievably stupid, though not so stupid she gave up covering herself entirely. He didn't laugh. She thought if he laughed she might kill him. But she felt so weak and she didn't understand why, deprived of shield, sword, moral superiority, even the righteousness of her own anger.

Without speaking, he let her pass. She wasn't sure if he did it to spare her (uncharacteristic of him), but she supposed, in his own way, he had—though neither did he give her whatever he carried (he wasn't even wearing it, it was folded over one arm, opposite his instrument). Most assuredly, she thought, so that he could watch her from behind as she left.

Gidian wondered if she was there; he could never tell. She wasn't particularly stealthy (she was), but being made of smoke, transparent as the sky, silent as the void, she'd never been easy to find. She represented so many things to him—beauty, potential, even things she wasn't, like the future—he couldn't stand confronting them, but did.

Gidian's life took place in bilateral compartments. There were two of him, and something like strangers, they only met at that moment the fields disappeared. Half a person with a hint of monster. He didn't have the stomach for beauty. No, that part of him drifted even now into sacred sky, his altar.

He wanted to cry. It was unmanly but he'd never been much of a man. Until now he'd made it up by not being a woman either, but what could he do? The warrior in him was dead; the poet.

Sarah moved silently, impossible to feel. And he wasn't sure, but he thought she liked to watch, when nobody knew, so more and more he made a show of himself to seem confident.... (some figure of a person, what fragment of a God) He couldn't help measuring against his monomial double: the warrior.

In her he experienced earthquakes of creation. She wasn't another person, she was himself and more of himself, bound by music, given ghostly frame, who thought and spoke separately—a girl. He wondered if she knew where she came from: hoped she didn't know she was a twin. He gave her rigorous, incestuous fatherhood. More and more the selfishness in him became self*less*ness, and he wasn't sure he liked that, because he couldn't recognize himself anymore.

At home he found his parents deep in discussion. Climbing upon eaves, he dropped: upon them talking about the children who had replaced him in the ritual; amazed, it seemed, that something, anything, had actually happened here. He threw a rock at the window—his solution, it seemed, for everything. In shattering, it replaced home with some place further, where reality wasn't.

So long he wandered; actuated to new meaning. He knew many songs, and they came easy as pure thought, perfect lightness. Many times he'd pondered drawing a map, but the idea seemed a parody of itself. While following (he split into two) he came upon his own ghost. The second sang harmony.

Scarred bronze lit the belly of the land; crushing dim his bedside candle. Lacquered clear the seeming state. Cutoff brass and knuckled fingers; delicate rise the rush and run. One place, where Gidian found himself, the river puddled into a deepish pool, big enough for swimming. On the bank he saw a big rock.

He wondered if she would come for him. Brave, strong (he pretended to be these things, for that same show), if he needed to, he could brave the dark. With a hammer, he could shatter these stones, and tear down mountains.

He sat there so long and she came.

Still silent and invisible, in the solarium rain, his awning. Even her blended sense. But sometimes he couldn't tell how much of her could be said to *exist*. Maybe he projected himself; the idea he could do that, that it could be done—and someplace, barely out of sync, a second number drew maps.

White lines sketched in to the color of skin, her familiar face. She looked confused; she always looked confused. The compound in her, a child, couldn't accept a stationary position: what he might call, if pressed, an identity. But even after so many thousand days of life, he still lost grasp of his own self. He felt like a group of people, but he only had one body.

He raised his arms, feeling like a pervert. Even fatherhood became incestuous in her presence. On occasion they occupied the same space. She slipped into him, her lack of presence to his vaginal aura. When they hugged, when he held her… if she wanted she wore him like a skin, maybe without him knowing, so close they were the same person again, pasted in air.

"I got you something." He pulled a length of cloth from his arms. A dress. "I found it below the river last night." He asked if she liked it and she nodded. If she could he thought she would speak to him. But inside, where were mistrust and vulnerability, he wondered if maybe she could speak already, and he just wasn't good enough. He suffered.

He handed her the dress. For a second it caught adrift, then fell, bypassing ligaments and fingers, into bellowing dust. He shook his head; and he wasn't sure, but it seemed she might be crying. So he picked it up, dusted it, unfolded it, and held it in profile against her.

White folds clung to her already (they'd been there since the beginning); whirled in an imaginary wind. He wasn't sure why, but he'd imbued her with a sense of his own modesty, one he only pretended to ignore. She didn't quite wear a dress, but it seemed a sheet almost, that kept her shape, and never flew away. He couldn't help admiring it. Her.

If she wanted, he said, he could take it somewhere for her—he could hang it on a tree, or put it somewhere for her to look at—until she could really wear it. He didn't want to admit his doubt that that day might ever come.

She nodded again. Maybe he imagined it, but she seemed to make quiet sounds. Her need—however internalized, another of his projections—pulled a cloud over him: a warm one. When he asked where she wanted him to take it, she blinked, squeezed her arms, shook her head, and gazed at his face, at war with something in one of them, he wasn't sure.

As they went, he imagined her hand in his. Almost like it was there.

They walked (he moved slower than her, carrying that baggage of the corpus) until they came to this beaten, mangled shell of a hut. It stank. Dead wood and collapsed ceiling. Fallen door and distraught presence. The leafless husk of a tree haunted the outside—corrosion.

"Is this where you live?"

Almost embarrassed, she nodded.

Inside, if you could call it that, he found a wretched thing of a table; broken windows. Overturned chairs against the far wall. His first step broke the boards, and his boot touched decrepit floor. Below the table, sick and oily, was a lump of what looked like uncooked bread.

"If you want," he said, "I could fix this place for you. Maybe. I wouldn't be very good at it, but I could try."

She smiled—that was good, he'd never gotten a smile before—and he spent the rest of the afternoon, not to mention many days afterwards, tearing down those same walls, throwing away, redecorating. He didn't know where to get new wood, so he tore down a whole shed, lacking the courage, at this point, to disassemble someone's actual *house*.

Sometimes she kept him company. Those were his favorite. She stood behind him, or beside him, one hand slipping *into* his arm. Nothing in life had prepared him for construction, but he braved it for her, chipping each day at a gigantic, unknowable block of ice. Taking breaks, he played her songs, and while working he whistled or sang. Like always, he idolized himself. He had songs for every occasion; songs to *become* the occasion. Even drained (sometimes he wasn't sure he'd be able to keep it up, without supplementing the drainage on his energy) he could still make beautiful music. The dress he'd hung on the tree outside. Admittedly it was scary, and the dress made the place look haunted, but he didn't care. He didn't care about anything anymore.

At night, he slept outside. Sarah lay beside him. Occasionally he saw her: white ghost in the dusk (she glowed); her paleness just beyond him. One night she'd even slept within him. Unwilling to go inside, they lay on the hill, facing away from the walls, not far away from his embryonic new creature, the dwelling at his back. Soon he could stand looking at it. At least that was a start. Evening, the sun painted heavy landscapes. Gidian had always considered the absence of light a density. During the day there were two of you: self and projection. Night pared them away. He didn't know how to exist in that species of void.

In this new person he became, he really did seem to be taking on the village's idea of symbols. He imagined sometimes that she was more real, but couldn't tell between sight and imagination, having already shorn between himself and the material, the psycho-presence he gave. Pure thinking become manifest in the external.

Thus he discovered paranoia.

One day something rustled outside their clearing. No one in the village would look for him, for a few days at least, quite simply because he did this all the time—so he imagined a whole militia of phantoms, ghosts and phantoms, to rustle those same leaves. Things in this world ate flowers: grotesque, inhuman, many-armed with red skin and protruding yellow eyeballs, icky film from them, creeping slowly from shadow to shadow, to shadow.

Or, even worse, it might have been Laura.

Waking, he rose into shuttered brightness—his eyes—and came to life outside the village. The hill had a steep slope (one night he'd rolled down it as he slept; woken inextricably tangled), but he'd become accustomed to gravity, and dispersed balance accordingly. First he stretched; next he squinted suspiciously at the bushes.

He'd never realized how exposed this place left him. A concentric awareness surrounded him, consumed him: spinning vantage, illusive. More and more he jumped at cracking twigs, swishing grass, wind (he imagined)—until he remembered that he *couldn't* be sneaked up on. If only that gave him more comfort. Obviously, if he were wrong, how could he possibly know?

Fear became ambiguity in him. Here there had never been anything to fear. Thus fear became distance and invisibility. He didn't know. Wishing sickness onto himself, wishing danger. No angle justified the things he felt. Maybe he imagined them. Maybe everything in the world, and the world outside, was nothing but a huge imagination. When he looked into the river, presence awash in reflection, his eyes glowed like burning moons.

At night, when it's quiet, I like to walk through the village. I don't need to see, so I see everything. When I think, I try to keep myself out of it. When I can help it, I don't refer to myself in the first person. But one day I realized I might not come back, and that meant I started asking if I had anything to come back to. I didn't know if I did.

I have a house now. I do my best to express gratitude. Not really so well, considering its silence, but father seems to understand. He cleaned up my last meal. He found a dress for me—not that I can wear it, but I can't live in my house either, and both of them make me happy, by association I suppose.

I just wish I could make *him* happy, by doing something other than being alive. I think there's a chance he might die soon, and I know why. There are more important things than me. When I'm gone, if I go, he'll still be here. Thus far this has been a guiltily one sided relationship.

I've always liked legends, not that that means anything considering my scale, considering I don't have one. They give me companionship because neither of us exist, and they help me replace myself. Immediately after happening *everything* becomes a story (legends being glorified stories). In a way, all existence is just a story that hasn't ended yet; or without beginning.

A few times I went to the hill when Jacob told his stories. I already knew them, obviously (I can be smart sometimes—really I know more than

I can keep track of, and that's the difficult part), but hearing them, even badly, they took on a new significance. There's a transition there: I've been looking for it. If I could just do that maybe then I wouldn't have to go.

No, I'm just trying to feel better. It isn't working.

I do like the new house. More than anything I like to stand in it. Light breaks through the ceiling (father hasn't gotten rid of the holes yet, but he will soon, and if he doesn't I don't care, I'm probably not worth it) and turns everything into a perfect cocoon, webs shining halos.

Sometimes I pretend to sleep. Sometimes I sleep next to him, inside him. He'd be warm if I could feel. I've never known what it means to be tired, and I haven't been hungry either. I don't like thinking about it. All I can do is imitate, and not very well either. It's impossible to juxtapose without understanding. I think.

There's this story I really like. Not many people know it because it contradicts everything else, or it's too complicated, I'm not sure. No matter how much the walls change they're still walls, and nothing, especially not a story, is allowed to go beyond that. I like the story because it makes me wonder, and I can relate to it. I guess it's the same way with all stories. It's about the sun, like most everything else, but it says different things about the sun, so the sun isn't the sun anymore, it's a *gateway*. But maybe I should tell it from the beginning, so it'll make some sense. Or a little, at least. I've never been able to stress context.

Once, a very long time ago, there used to be an old man. He was old, and bald, and wrinkled, and long life had made him shorter. Both his children were dead, and his friends, and his grandchildren thought he was frightening, so he didn't see them either. He'd outlived himself in an even older land, even if by extension, this being a legend, that meant the land was young.

This man spent his life walking through the village. It's what we all do when we're young, but when we get older we stop moving, having houses now, and gardens, and children, and we move vicariously through them, directing. The soreness built up in his joints, but it went away when he walked enough. He said it was why he'd lived to be so old, but he didn't know. Like most people he had two legs, hands, eyes, feet, matching toes and fingers, but he fancied himself a theologian, or a storyteller, if our village can differentiate between them. The priest disapproved of him (I always wonder if the priest was Jacob's great grandfather to some gigantic exponent; he certainly *sounds* like the same person, and when I think of him I think of Jacob's father), but sometimes the children gathered around to hear him tell stories, and they liked his stories because they'd never heard them before.

While walking, he thought. Occasionally inspiration came to him; after so many thousand days of slow inspiration he'd lived a *life* of inspiration.

One day the man discovered a means of seeing closer. Water, he thought, magnified proportion, but what would happen if water looked *through* water, as another solid? So he took the water and made it solid by sorcery, and layered it, and put it to his eyes, and he saw new creases.

He walked for a long time seeing into hard water. Then one day he decided he didn't want his original vision, so he took out his eyes and replaced them with clear magnifying orbs: he called them glasses. And he still walked around the village everyday, but when children saw him coming they ran, and he didn't like being run from, and he avoided them all he could. It made him so sad he didn't care to see them at all.

He kept walking, but the village he loved didn't exist anymore, its unity broken into ugly fragments. So he tried to shut his eyes, but he couldn't, and he went mad, and not so long after he died. But before he died, when he was still caught up in his madness, taking momentary pity, for fear of bad spirits, the villagers took him to a podium by the main houses—his sepulcher—and fed him everyday, so they could hear him rambling, and frothing, and screaming.

He said "goliath" "the blasphemer" that he'd looked up, and now he'd seen the sun "bleeding fire" for "a screaming": it saw like he did, he said, "in pieces," and it couldn't possibly love them, "the creatures." He'd seen closer than any man alive, "by diving," and if he didn't love them neither could the sun, after "the Endless Day." And then he died.

The children feared him because as he looked into the sun the glass magnified the inside of his skull, shining lights in it. Sinking blue and hollow bones of the skull. No one knew what he'd seen, because no one knew how to freeze water, but they did know what they saw *in* his eyes; and if he was right about magnification and perspective, if they both worked the same, what did they see magnified as they looked into the *sun*?

Our past is all around us, in us, about us, and almost all our legends take place in the village, or in identical places that are really the village projected. Story has its root in experience, whether addressing or remembering. The conceptual gains weight by virtue of influence. Self acclimates understanding; projects onto the invisible. Everything in the world, one might say, is invisible. Solid channels abstraction. History, values, and customs are invisible. Humanity itself is invisible, half in, half out of the solid universe.

Story is invisible.

It helps me prove myself, to myself, and I feel smarter. When I focus I stop sounding like myself because I'm not confused anymore. That's part of what I meant when I said I could relate. I'm also used to people not understanding me, but mostly just because they don't know I exist.

Another interesting thing about the story is that it has a sad ending. Most of our legends end with a triumphant victory: the hero climbs over the wall, gets carried to meet the Sun God, or the Sun God comes to him. It's probably why people forgot the story, but also the reason I remembered it. It's so unlike most legends that maybe, just maybe, it might be true.

But sometimes I realize that if I wanted, I could find out. As much as I'd like to be, I'm *not* human, especially because I can fly. Jacob walks up stairs but I don't even need them. I think about it and I get scared, but looking up, the sky seems familiar. Sometimes I dream of coming down from it. For some reason, in these dreams I tend to be naked.

I think my health might be getting worse. If I breathed I would be having trouble. It scares me. I always figured being immaterial has its advantages, but the softest wind might blow me away, soul made of dust and clear feathers. Father doesn't like to mention it but I can see inside his mind. It's no use being afraid but sometimes I just can't help it.

Last night, before the sun set, I went to the hill. I know I shouldn't have but I couldn't help that either, and there wasn't anyone to stop me, other than myself. The whole way I had to listen to the most annoying scolding. Me at my least charming.

Dusk peeled in layers; low gates leading nowhere. Imagining footsteps, I led an immense army, of only one member. Snowflake souls rose, escaping before night. The other parts of me couldn't stop arguing, like always, but I did my best to ignore them. From one side, stalks leaned to block my way. From the other, an equal force assisted.

It isn't true that others make it inside. Sometimes they cross the gates, but they don't go anywhere. There are two hills in the center of our village: one inside it; another opening into some empty field. That barrier only opens to a few people at a time (three or four, in alternation), and until they get too old, no one else can get inside.

Hazy orange like an overripe melon: the closer I got, the more I saw it. It was tall, and straight, and black; harsh angled, four cornered; rectangular darkness, connecting earth to sky. Something in it, some pattern, made it transparent when you were far enough away, but in proximity it grew solid—not density, but an absolute *absence* of space, inside which nothing existed.

At the bottom, I saw it led directly into the sun. When I touched it, it felt like cold, cold glass.

Laura arrived home to find Michelle asleep in a pile on the couch, upon which she ran inside, past her, up the stairs, and the creaking floor came behind her. She dressed very quickly, though she couldn't help missing the dress she'd lost. It had been her favorite.

Life had new singular patterns. Waking, she rose into that same alien landscape, except it was just her alien room, distant and unreachable. A honeycomb fallout, tessellation in rhomboid chambers. Her ghost didn't belong here anymore, but there were more of her, so many she didn't know where to find Laura, her one true essence, in the three dimensional lie.

She rarely left the house, meaning she spent most her time alone. After so long thinking of Michelle as a form of decoration (on the couch, at the table; unfortunately, the kind that talked), it was odd seeing how wrong she'd been. Her parents still hadn't reappeared. Wherever she went she found Gidian, and she couldn't help thinking, really, it was better to put off *that* conversation for later.

All her life, in the space around her house, she'd grown a garden—in her own, somewhat biased opinion, perhaps the finest in the village. Especially now, she filled it with flowers. In her youth the flowers had spoken to her: white winds, streaking silver wings. She hoped with all of herself that just stepping out the door wouldn't bring Gidian to her.

She became a current within the floral furnace. Around her rose specks of energy, immaterial slip from many petals, and further rose thin strings, never tangling, from the back of every villager, channeling that same energy in the ganglia. In her mind she danced, to know the presence of her own children.

Laura didn't often sing, but she sang now. Her pitch came true, and she had a good voice. Not as good as Gidian, but she wasn't thinking about him, so she pretended not to make the comparison. Presence dispersed outwards; and for brief moments, flickers taking place in the subconscious, she knew what it meant to be immaterial, to leave and return (soul without body) from the world, without having to live in it, puzzle in it, suffer in it. In her more sentimental moments she wished she were a leaf on a tree: that when she fell, her life would fall with her, until destiny buried her in footprints.

The sixth day Michelle noticed Laura had become furniture. She asked why. Laura attempted to flick her away, like a sneeze, and when that didn't work she decided to ignore her, not realizing that she didn't *know* why. Her second, third, and fourth selves, not to mention the first, were nowhere to be seen.

"This probably isn't healthy," Michelle said. "You'll turn into a cushion."

"Go away." Laura threw a pillow at her. "Come back when I start to care."

Of course, she thought, where *could* she go? Normally her day began with an escape into unreality, segueing into a long, long walk. Before, she'd never realized how disconnected that made her. But she didn't enjoy being furniture, and she'd never liked this place much anyway.

In newly discovered paranoia, at every step she feared a follower. Heavy fruit hung. One she picked, and the branch rustled, starting a wave-like flow that went on for *far* longer than strictly necessary. Was it possible, she wondered, that she had an invisible brocade of mutant followers, many chambered eyes her refracted glint?

She ate the fruit as she walked. Her need for secrecy took control, anchored in the binary. Leaves drenched peripheral vision. Taste came crisp, sweet, delirious. As she chewed, she was careful to sift the seeds out of her mouth. All her life, for real, she'd been scared that if she swallowed one it would take root in her stomach, until it grew out her hands, her feet, her mouth, and she'd be a piece of little girl with a tree in her, grotesque symbiote till the trunk burst her lungs....

A distant sun watched her every move, magnified it. It centered her holy triune background. The sun hung absolutely untouchable; the walls could be touched, but not crossed; the gardens so close, so touchable, as to be almost unfair.

Balance, she thought. Somehow they equalized, prioritized, channeled.

She walked along the walls. Angling her head correctly, she could see all three at once. The combination was too much: saturated in the sterile kinetic. At her feet, the same rock crumbled. She searched the walls for the cave. She didn't expect it to be there, but she felt obligated. In a way, coming here with Jacob had changed her life; just she didn't much care, and she forgot him easily. When he left, he'd taken the cave with him. They were a part of each other (Jacob and cave, cave and Jacob), and he belonged there, much as he belonged anywhere. More than anything he didn't belong here. If he came back she'd welcome him, and if he was better he'd be Jacob again, but she wouldn't dignify him for leaving, not after the time she spent looking for him. He didn't merit the effort.

Apathetic, she passed along crest, lateral to churning columns. Strong face in the rock, uncle and father. They rose, mediated the village. And for a moment she wondered what it would be like *without* the wall. In their centered, regulated, timeless world. The sun shone too beautiful; it gave them light. What, in its bastard cousin, could equalize? She wished to be in a different field, on a hill unbearably close to the sun, but to stay there forever this time, where existence remained absolutely new, and the gardens hadn't grown yet, and there was the silhouette of a phoenix carved on the wall... not that she knew what that meant. She had dreams of flying—not away from the village but above it, seeing in combination. Up close everything mattered, the houses and gardens, but pulling away the village became a map of itself, aloft in cacophonous pillars....

Maybe she'd been dreaming *too* much recently. She dreamed of comic monsters, her friends in weird reinterpretation—grotesque eyes, longer teeth, big noses, even larger hats, triumphant entrance onto an absolute dimension. Way down in that clear piece of crystal, glass refracted her semblance of consciousness, and without an anchor (soul to body) she saw so many monsters; naked, elongated; those other versions she kept on a shelf for more demanding occasions... and above it stood yet another, the malicious one, grinning evilly on a stage full of puppets, strung upwards to the sun, holding a gigantic pair of scissors. If she drew a circle then she drew it: traced in air. Long hair and aura of the gentle mother; she wore glorious robes draped like waterfalls.... She was a waterfall, of energy surging to earth, turning stones to diamonds....

She kicked another rock, the same. The wall became a tapestry, laced in rainbows. Way to the left—she kept the wall on the right, circling east to west—dove pristine peaks (the river), silver highway 'cross lower levels; in the ground, beneath infinite stones, above pendulous labyrinths. And in the center, with nowhere to go, stood Laura, feeling very small despite beautiful hair, crushed by a million unknowns, an iceberg.

So she walked even slower. No matter what, she only went in a circle, meaning she never went anywhere. That used to be enough, but she couldn't tell anymore if she'd matured (she doubted it), or if everything else had gotten smaller, a collapsing molecule in her timeless dimension....

Ahead, she saw (barely), a bit inland on the left, something shaped like a dwelling. She'd come by many, ignoring them. Such buildings were usually abandoned for their position near the walls, in want of proximity to the center of the village. Small children feared them. In the past, villagers had used them to store things people had forgotten. But this one seemed different, she realized, because it had a flag, or something like that, that hung off a tree.

It stood atop a broad, shallow hill. Around that grew tall stalks of some plant she didn't recognize: fruitless, but it had long, full leaves, and many of them; pale yellow, thin and dry. The more she saw of the dwelling, the uglier it grew. It seemed to have fallen apart lifetimes ago. Rotten wood piled to either side. Come close enough (she denied it as long as she could, making excuses, proclaiming it impossible), she saw that what she'd originally called a flag had been her *dress.*

Very swiftly she slipped into the flora. Tough leaves cut at her. Whoever lived here, what ungodly pervert; she didn't know whether it scared, repulsed, or angered her. She probably should have run, but she couldn't ignore a very powerful obligation, above everything else, to get her dress back (she didn't know where she got her priorities from, but maybe it would undo her adventure the other day) and, if possible, get revenge on whoever had taken it.

Like her own allegorical shadow, she crept. Lacking talent, she rustled leaves, but it didn't matter this far away. Most probably this would ruin the dress she wore, so it became a holy crusade, article for an article—unfathomable. She channeled adrenaline, feeling, on some strange level, that this was the most important thing she'd ever done.

Getting there took longer than it probably should have. She'd been right about the dress. Only some miracle kept it in place. By that same miracle, the leaves didn't harm her skin, despite itchiness. Vengefully, she wished she'd brought a weapon—and for some reason, the idea seemed less ridiculous than it sounded. More than once she scolded herself for not being prepared.

However long after, feeling a desperate urge to sneeze, she stood outside the clearing. It looked even worse, despite patches of newer wood. Inside lived skeletons. She paid close attention; then crouched because standing at an angle became uncomfortable. Most that time she spent making plans. Few took into consideration her lack of physical strength, and combat experience.

On the other side, someone began hammering. Unfortunately, he'd gotten to her weapon first, which might have saved his life. She assumed him male; this place had little of the feminine about it, as did stealing dresses, though she supposed, if she was wrong, life had thrown larger surprises at her.

The hammering stopped. Footsteps. They sounded like masculine footsteps, to make the distinction. She crouched, baring claws, forgetting how ridiculous she looked. She wasn't sure, but even without a face she might hate him.

Gidian walked around the corner. He spoke gently under his breath. Moments later he began singing. Laura didn't know what to think: and in a similar state, frozen as anything could be while still being alive, she watched him without breathing. He picked up a board and went around the corner again.

She stayed that way, closer and closer to suffocation, until, having lost track of the physical, she sneezed. The hammering stopped. She gasped, fumbled, choked. Without thinking (less brave than before despite the absence of fear—tentativeness, maybe) she dashed quickly to the dress: grabbed it, and ran very, very fast.

Gidian squirmed in his coat. After so long in the wilderness (one might call it that), the coat felt greasy, dirty, and gross. Within it he ought to be masculine, but he shivered. He knew nothing of cold, but everything of its substance. For days, despite Sarah—because of her—it was almost as though he'd been alone.

He thought of walking, and for the first time in days he left the shack. His hands hurt. His muscles couldn't take the strain of lifting, and for some reason that scared him. Was he so frail, he wondered, that he couldn't even build a house? (Though when he repeated the question, it didn't sound so bad.)

Trees passed, as though they were the ones moving. Gidian had transcended the most noticeable aspects of self; replaced them with unity. She equaled him, and they wove together, even if he couldn't tell himself apart. It seemed that way.

He suffered.

They strode parallel to the river. Even direction meant nothing. Where two went there could be more, or one, or none, and did he belong there? His mind and his replacement of the hammer. Ripples in lucid patterns. Grandiose designs he became them.

Inspecting his reflection, he suffered. Normally he'd write a song about himself, for being handsome, but he couldn't do that now. For one he didn't have his instrument (that mattered), but more than that he wasn't so sure about the handsome. His tangled hair and the grime he'd swallowed; the uneven space they took together.... He felt too much like the shadow of a person, unwilling to dirty hands in his own pockets. He didn't have his good pants, nor, more importantly, his hat. The boots he'd abandoned.

Suddenly he felt very lost, having lost not only his first, but also his second self. What had he gotten in return? Destiny fed him on diets of the invisible, yet it was stingy on that too.

"Sarah?" he said, looking up. Without the strength to verify it, he felt as though he were crying. "I think I'll go home for a day. I'll be back," he hung his head, "but I just need to take a break." He heard nothing, like always. Her signs and sense of presence were there.

But when he turned, they were all she'd left behind.

::::::::::::::::::::

At home—still unpleasantly familiar—he grabbed more clothes; wore them. He'd stopped at the river to bathe (modest for fear of invisible eyes), after returning to the shack for instrument, boots, and hammer. He picked them up in that order, but it didn't feel right. Normally he never would have taken the instrument first. In denial he told himself he'd missed it, but in reality, he liked to save the best for last.

For the first time, he wished that he had a younger sibling, that he might bully them. He thought of making music, but he was too tired, he told himself. Bright colors infuriated him. The couch didn't feel right, compared to grass. He suffered.

A middle-aged couple ran past his window, looking somewhat ruffled. He'd seen them on occasion, visiting somewhere down the road. Apparently they'd smiled too much for one day, and had just now gotten over it. They had matching brown hair. Whenever they came (Gidian really did see them frequently, either out walking or in [out] this very same window) they held hands, one standing a few feet ahead like contenders in a mystery race to nowhere.

Gidian's own parents came home soon. They looked equally cheerful, and he wanted to throw something at them. His father's nose, cheek, and brow glowed bright pink; he hadn't noticed it before, but his mother was gaining weight. Somewhere sensitive, he grew less fond of his hair for being the same shade as theirs. But at least he didn't have a mustache.

Much too energetically, they told him about the initiation ceremony for the new children. There was nothing he wanted to hear less. He screamed. They said they'd let a friend borrow one of his hats (some toddler he didn't care to know—by friend they meant *their* friend's children), and he screamed some more.

Tonight they would be having soup for dinner.

:::::::::::::::::::

Where do babies come from?

They grow on stems, and when we want one, we pick them.

:::::::::::::::::::

Aqua fingernails, dirt beneath them. They pricked strangely, causing infection. Tendons led back to palm, forearm, bicep and shoulder, acid fang and purple muscles in the neck. Gidian's monster looked like a fever-dream fantasy. It behaved like the monster in a children's story, but eviler.

Shudders threw him from dreams. Red curtains slapped him in the face. Very possibly, in the history of the village, barring concussion and Jacob, he'd become the first person to ever take a nap. The strangeness didn't register until he saw gold outside diving onto the neighbor's roof: a shingle. The shock didn't come until he realized why this felt so unfamiliar.

He stood, fetching instrument and hat, and left the house. Already it tired him, and he hated his parents more than ever. Boisterous, flabby, flatulent presences. His mother's cooking had never been particularly good, and his father, whether he believed it or not, had nothing to do with his son's musical genius.

For some reason, more prominent even than the urge to flatten the nightstand, he wanted to jump over a fence. Not just any fence, but an outdoor fence. He didn't know where he would find one, but somewhere out there, not so far away, was a fence, *the* fence, *his* fence.

Long ago, in miniaturized times before puberty, he'd called them hurdles, and hurt himself whilst hurling. Long after, called from dreams, he would rise to that challenge, bearing boot and wooden instrument, flamboyance and guile. His trickery might be of little use, but he would use it anyway, and his fencing skills were out of the question (he didn't have any), but he would use those too. Melodramatic flames sprouted from the void between nostrils. Fever fumed in hollow temple: knock and his skull made a sound like dropped logs.

Out the door—it shut with the sound of splitting logs—he beat percussion into passage, marching tall and proud. He didn't look like a soldier, but instead the perfect *imitation* of a soldier, threatening enough to scare small animals and banish little sisters to the end of the world, where they sleep on gravel that makes them cry.

Before he found the fence he found a bush, stopping to ask directions. It pointed to the left, right from the left, left to right, in that direction, and he saluted like the gentleman his mother hoped he would be. Arriving there—the right—he spoke at length to a stump, learning much; maybe exhausting his welcome, the rigid thing didn't have the complex to give directions: learning little.

Beneath a tree, he sunned in the shade. Long limbs grew smoother, and he couldn't help admiring his own nakedness. Soon afterwards he grew unbearably self-conscious, whereupon he proceeded to dress, wallow, and cry. His personal demons trailed mercilessly, always on the hunt. When he brought them fruit they wanted vegetables, but that wasn't enough either; they wanted fruit *and* vegetables, just they didn't want to tell him out loud.

When he found the fence he took his vengeance like a monster. First he pounded with a sword, to break it—splinters and torn fingers—then, when that only worked a little, he kicked it, and knocked it down, and stepped on it. Then he jumped over it, over and over and over, and did a dance for victory.

::::::::::::::::

Once, a long time ago, he'd stood alone in a clearing, wearing clothes. He felt a breeze so there must have been something wrong. Seeing himself, he realized, the memory must be all wrong, he actually stood *outside* himself. He wondered if that was possible. He had his arms raised as he played a song. The words weren't the same but he couldn't help rearranging. He'd worked on this song for ever, even before he discovered music, and what else could he do? Difference between better and worse didn't mean anything in the cold outside. By reaching into a deep well, it just meant he opened doorways. He hadn't made it perfect yet, but he hadn't finished either; rolling water becomes flying flower, becomes waving wind, becomes tone and voice. Jacob rolls down the hill and he catches that too. Gidian hadn't rolled for a million days, he told himself. Different viewpoints he added, Laura still speaking about flowers: he saw her, he saw her, and he saw. Repeated themes echo in the underlying structure, still building for whatever refrain, if the song has one. He doesn't know himself, but that doesn't stop it from happening: thought never stopped anything from happening, except maybe action, and there were times Gidian didn't see what impact that had on anything that mattered. Gidian had never considered himself a poet, whatever he told himself. The artist mindset and an aura of arrogance: he learned them from himself, disproving singularity. Righteous timbres hit, and totality becomes something equivalent to rain.

:::::::::::::::::

He dreamed Sarah let go her shroud. She had clear skin just like his, identically pale; if they became light then no one would know, they were that shade already. Her fingers turned time outside, pointed in five directions like a star; waved slowly past, trailing water. They drifted underwater, he realized. Somewhere empty where textures were like water, and space became liquid glass. Her image glowed hyper real, super clear about the edges. Texture and breath spun clarity. Foam fell worlds away.

He touched her, and his fingers passed *through her,* into her. Her image rippled like part of that same pool of water. Colorless space at her back; rushing inward a fountain. No, without ever leaving place, her ward and wings they shivered. He didn't ripple with her (clear blue backdrop) but *he* rippled as she hung in place, wind and blessing.

A black funnel formed in the space behind her, whorled spin about it. Vectored lightning: born, lived and died in its womb. When the next generation came their column spun laterally like whirlpools. Flooding frames grew to taller objects. Pendulous light shined from her. This time she touched him, reaching in for his heart, still moving chest and puerile being. Her hand unlidded a geyser, and raw energy shot out, a rush of fluttering wings.

Undecided on a whisper, he sighed declarations of love. This whole universe was submerged under water. Whatever distant, incomprehensible universe. Movement within: a flow to other regions, congealing unanimity. He swum, and as he swam they sank (they had always been sinking), but they sank together into the inky core of that oyster centrifuge. Shimmering in light, she grew even more beautiful up close.

I can't stand the feeling that when I walk, I'm not going anywhere. Motion seems optional (I float like clothes on a wire, dance like them), but when I fall out of sync, it's like being torn. I'm fragile, I guess, and I don't have the constitution for pain. Does that make me weak? Sometimes I can' help feeling like a little girl, even if I'm not one.

Twin peaks arched together, framed against lightning. I walked beneath them—or I floated; imagining, no really feeling, that I hung like a puppet on a cord, its root anchored in my stomach—onto a monstrous plateau, jutting into furious clouds.

Wind whipped my clothes, ripping white strands to lateral banding. I held them to maintain a simulacrum of balance, or prevent floating—because yes, I might be lifted by the wind, that its grasping claws seize me, that I whirl in its hands.

Without realizing it, I'd left the village, and gone where you could see the storm. But it didn't storm in the village. Was it possible that even though it looked the same, it might not *be* the same?

I don't sleep, and I've never had a dream, so I couldn't know. Sometimes, coming back after falling apart, I'm not where I remember myself being. Maybe that resembles sleep, or the feeling of waking up, but inversely. Instead of journeying into myself—embryonic flake in that clear piece of crystal—I break consciousness and semblance of body, becoming others.

More than anything I worry about meeting myself, another part of myself, who refuses to become me again. If they had the constitution to leave, I probably wouldn't want them in the first place—but what if, along with themselves, they'd taken something with them? I'm too selfish to let them take the things I think are mine, even if it belongs to them too.

Raising my arm, shroud became feathers and wing; dualistic, I sprouted another... I didn't need wings to fly, just like I don't need legs to walk, or a body to live, but they helped, and I wouldn't feel comfortable without them. Recently I'd been putting belief in the material. Maybe it would do a favor for me.

Flying upwards, I rediscovered the funnel there, slinging torpor, spitting hail. It gurgled tornadoes, spilling horror from gaping fuligan jaws: singularity in absence, nonexistence breeching the fundamental solid.

I was just a meal to this sludge filled monster, drainage tube for the fecal matter of all universes—so small I became something without taste, but must be consumed regardless.

It roared for me.

It lunged, dark enough that had there been a sun, it would have been swallowed. Proportion lurched, shredded in a spatial gate, and its hoary bulk seemed to collapse around me—not an approach but a recession, blocking out sound and warmth and wind. White traces (the flickers of lightning) receded to a ring around the edge; disappeared entirely.

It came.

I dove into the ground, escaping from direction as though into a separate body of water. Many colors flared: red background with flickers of gold; a purplish landscape; a riotous sea—I passed through each, in the zones of no rupture. They had the softness, the transparency of blankets. There might have been many, but it felt like only one, or two, lying atop the same object, that did not move, and had never done so.

Birthing light split my world in half, a harsh glare in ovoid chambers—and yes, I *opened* my eyes. Sharp breathing burrowed tunnels to my ears, punching tickets against the vibrating mechanism; unfurling lungs replenished me.

But no, I just have an active imagination—that sometimes I wish I could get rid of. In this life I've gone many places, but I can never tell where I go, and when I get back, even more goes from me: first the sense of *having traveled*, and then the secondary sense of having gone there too. Being myself, and many other people, I pretend I've gotten used to it, but I never have.

The hill sloped down to a field of grasses, where I pretended to be, though I wasn't. Even with father's lessons on presence (he taught without speaking), and my attempts to be a good student, nothing moved for me. I felt myself in many other places, cut off from any single moment when all moments are singular. I missed father, but he said he'd be back soon, and I believed him. I always believed him, despite his not being very trustworthy, because he was a part of me too, and that voice, the silent one, spoke from a place inside my many selves, that I'd like to think would be free of lies. It wasn't necessarily so, but I knew that too.

Everything lurched when I pretended to stand, and already I'd lost track of location. The nearest path was yellow and soft. It led to the wasteland, and had come from there also. I left no marks in it; soon I came to a place that wasn't a place. Without a purpose it had died, lay dead, and been forgotten. That bled into me unpleasantly. There couldn't be two of us.

And so, only moments later, I was somewhere else: gentle roofs amidst specialized gardens, with curled fruit growing in them, and ripe vegetables in hung clusters, all so beautiful it might have sprouted this morning. In the rest of the village, plants reproduce and bear fruit within days, but unpicked crop lasts for much longer. The outsides turn dark, the insides heavy with sweet liquid. But this was something else entirely.

This was Laura's house, and her garden—not to mention her neighbors, inside their own houses, but in a sense the neighbors also belonged to themselves. The vicinity took pride by association, and pretended to own it; but no, really she owned them, and she always would.

Laura stood in her garden. Stalks tangled at her feet, exchanging radiant energy. Maybe she didn't know, as a matter of scale, but she was their personal altar, exalting self and universe, channeling essence. Inside (more and more, I *saw* inside her) she mothered dimensions, a carrier of stars. All existence has the same basic material, unrefined to the microscopic degree, fluctuating on phase. When Laura moved, she ignited subtle changes in that fundament. When it returned, she brought return to earlier timeless states.

I found myself getting jealous. It wasn't fair that we should have the same hair, the same face and arms, yet only she got to be real. In lightness, attaining ephemeral grace, she might have been weightless. And no, I've never thought of myself as being jealous, but much of that comes from having nothing to lose.

In all of us there is a monster

Invisible clouds formed a spheroid chamber around her, weightless as any unseen object. Golden wings took on an electron orbit; culminated to a single glowing beam. She lifted both arms. She danced without moving. Existence danced around her: sustenance and center. I'd never, in all my life, been so jealous. She barely realized it happened, but she did so much, while I did so little. Her eyelashes fluttered, and her dress blew, whipping at angles. She wore my dress, even if it had been hers first. I wondered: did that count? I couldn't touch it, couldn't wear it, had no use for it, but it needed to be mine. It gave me many things invisible. I think I might have hated her, just a little, even if on more levels than one (I didn't like to admit it, and ironically, she didn't know) she happened to be my mother.

I couldn't help it, but I screamed at her. My screams shift invisible particles. It made a noise silently, and she heard it. Everything spun so loud—no one knows, but the world is loud, beneath a million roaring layers—I couldn't have known, but she heard it, and she turned to me, and she saw me, and our eyes were the same eyes (light turquoise blue). I couldn't help being the image seen in the mirror.

I've never been good at thought, but I'm unmatched in my ability to disappear. I did. Helix streams became field and sky. This time, I realized, I really *was* over the village. Only the river had shape; texture became flatness and lumps. Luckily, I've never had a fear of heights, or falling. It's convenient being able to fly.

I've always lived sporadically, but I wish I had a better understanding of place. The further I go the less real I become. Solid shape is an aspect of the singular. I would rather be a rock, I think, than populate entire planets. I'm beginning to get on my own nerves.

I flew for a while, and then I fell: spasmodic breach past shifting frequencies. Having never appreciated beauty, nothing changed now. Doubt made me bitter, and continued to do so.

As I get older, day by day I've discovered bitterness. I'm not sure I like it, but it seems necessary to the continuation of existence, even one like mine.

Flying lower—I made sure not to be higher than the walls, to keep myself from seeing out—I saw Laura's house again. She stood without seeing, one hand above the flowers. Confusion became her, and frailty accompanied presence. From this distance, despite myself, I began to love her.

I thought of returning, but I couldn't. I think this was what it felt like to be embarrassed. Could it really be that one and one, equaling two, equaled none? I knew already, but I've never been good at answering questions.

The closer I got to the sun, the closer then to flame. Heat seared my imaginary wings. It was always hot in the village, more so now than ever before. If I flew long enough, chances were I might burn, and fall like a comet, and explode with a shower of dust....

I landed on a hill. My hill. The house posed strangely, still incomplete. Father was many things, but he would never be a carpenter. Coming here, and seeing it now, I realized that though he might return, he would never finish anything. A skeletal tree, bony fingered with charred wood for the nails, naked in daylight, usurped as gravestone. There were many things to forget. Necessity happened to be among them. Existence crumpled under accumulation, bearing that weight of necessity: became lightness, dispersing. To be, one violates nonexistence, becoming solid. I'm not sure what that means but by necessity it affects me, whole pressurized oceans of the invisible.

I'm not sure, but I think I left. Dislocated, I undertook many journeys—seeing inside minds, replacing myself with them. Emerging from darkness I re-became that darkness, fulminating in long bands across a clear sheet of images; that sheet was the sky, and those bands the elongated semblance of a soul, threaded in specious dimension, dredging the flyways. I barely possess faculties of memory; barely possess anything at all, like a loosely tied bundle of sticks from which many have slipped already. Again I attempted to reassign myself, imagining senses, not knowing what to look for, never finding them. Nearby spread many paths. Above towered an octoid darkness, nonexistence, an ultimate barrier. I stood close enough to see it so I must have been by the center of the village. Stalks poked through what ought to have been my torso. Walking, I pretended to move them.

I emerged near the entrance. The gates looked something like a temple, surrounded by a large clearing. Evening shadows grew deep and heavy. Stone benches (older than memory) seemed randomly dispersed, yet impossible to move. On one sat a little girl—I recognized her. She was one of the three new children, extremely young. She had short auburn hair, not so different from her bronzed skin, that curled just above her neck. She wore a thin gown, and held her knees together. Hands she pressed to her face. She cried softly, but with long sobs. Her tears shone on her cheeks, more at the top of her gown. I wanted to comfort her, but when I put my hand on her shoulder it went right through, and when I told her everything would be all right she couldn't hear. I didn't know why she cried, but I felt what she felt, and the more I thought about it, the more I thought about myself, I realized soon I might be crying too.

Living in a post-traumatic universe, with even vengeance gone, Laura's life had become very boring. The valley had never been so warm, nor so small. She took walks during the day, but she never went anywhere. Nor did she brave the river.

Like an old person, she watched children play. They disgusted her, by being naive. Had she ever been like that? (She was afraid to answer the question because she already knew). A long time ago, in a hazy, hazy place, where she was even more of a little girl, what had given constitution to her pitiful universe?

She'd even glimpsed the three children. It hadn't been very long (less than twenty days ago, but more than five, or ten) but already they'd been there forever, one having become the focal point she herself had always been. On a gigantic scale they gave the village purpose, but she couldn't put faith in that now. She wanted to, but never again.

Her second self made the trail she followed: in dreams, on walks in the garden. Alone, she lost awareness of herself; outside found the loneliness still there. She didn't know where it went, her daemon, but it fed her shadows, and gave her entropy. Frequently she cried without realizing her own tears.

Suddenly, without reason, she missed Jacob. He never had to think, and he gave that to her; helped her forget that she didn't much like him. But Jacob, in his new entirety, constituted an absence, and she had nothing to measure him against but that hole. He'd always been about becoming someone else, to replace whatever life he did have, and his only personality came from old stories—but what if he hadn't carried her at all (she didn't even think he was strong enough), but something *else*, some mystery, had done it for them…? Maybe she trusted her dreams too much, assuming that just because they came from herself, it ought to be good advice, but she doubted it. She hadn't seen anything but what she'd expected to see: an older, stronger version of Jacob, without counterpart in the outside.

In opposition to morning, the sun became a shutting eye. Flowers shut too, conserving energy throughout the night. Even this early, she weakened. No one could be outside at night unless they had the Sun God's permission; or, paradoxically, if they'd already been out the night before. In stories, that permission came as a miniature replica of the sun, encased behind lamp-like glass, which fed life in the absence of the real sun, but burned out in the morning. That had never made sense to her, if anything just because she had no idea how to request such a blessing. Only Jacob's father cared enough to enforce the rules. But was it possible that somewhere, in a place no one ever saw, there was something that stayed out *every* night?

Her journey took her past benches, flowers, an abandoned blanket, hills, grass, fruit, gardening utensils, the walls, houses, half a fruit, footprints, the fading sky, the river, columns carved of light, but nothing that hadn't been her life up until now. She cared for nothing she found there. Not now. Maybe never.

Her attention drifted to facets of motion: swinging arms, legs, feet, her rustling dress, quiet breath, combination with gravity, newborn weariness, even the continual weight of just *being*. But nothing by which she might judge, assess, analyze. The roaring sun, feeling of wearing skin. It meant little as a falling stone, and landed without echo. So similarly: practiced step and progress without echo. Inconsequentially she made her way, absolutely unimportant, like a sound with no one to hear. Dispersing balance took her forward. Her second, third, fourth, and twenty-filth selves passed judgments; she turned and they fell silent, without echo.

Wood cracked up ahead. She crept forward, forgetting to leave the path. Wind blew in her ears—she imagined. She narrowed her eyes, claws extended; hid in a bush at the edge of the wasteland. Beyond it, Gidian performed a duet with the wall: hitting it with an already mutilated club, smirking. Between flails his hair shook.

Laura had expected something like this—Gidian had never dealt with stress well. But never, ever, would she have guessed that piece of wood to be his instrument, as she saw: subtle thwack of broken strings, hollow crunch in fiber body.

Just as obvious: much of that time, he hadn't been there. His soul, the most important part, seemed barely a spectator.

She marveled.

Gidian swung, tossed, and crunched; then, tossing the wreck to the ground, hurled himself against the wall as though to hurl *through* it. Skull met stone with a vengeance, ricocheted and fell to the ground. He squirmed for many moments, screaming. Then he tried again, this time to climb. He got past the height of his own body before Laura threw a rock at him. The rock hit him firmly on the spine.

He fell.

Laura waited for him to move. He didn't, and she poked him with a stick. He grumbled. She poked him again and he snorted. A third try and he grabbed for the stick, missed, and spasmed. Laura hoped it hurt, more now than before, with him awake to experience the pain.

"Sarah?" She shook her head.

She poked him again. Hard.

"Why do you keep calling me that?" she asked.

Gidian's head was more lump than skull. She poked him there, and he cried out in pain.

He ignored her question. Instead, he said: "My head hurts."

"You bashed it against the wall a little while ago," she pointed out. "Then I hit you in the back with a rock, because you took my dress."

"I did?"

"And then you hung it on a tree, because you're insane. Really."

He did a good job pretending he hadn't known. But gradually she had to tell him what he'd done. Not long after that, he began to cry.

She didn't know if he'd ever stop.

::::::::::::::::::

She left him there: avenged, even if she wasn't proud, and she hadn't meant to take that vengeance. Night sank about her, and she sank with it, gently to a coral powdered abyss. Heavy water crushed at the shell of an entropic universe. In tandem, 'midst gaseous clouds, 'neath towers of ocean, she pressed four limbs into gumlike existence—it absorbed her.

Far away, as the sun fell, she fell with it; illumination ran from her. She stumbled onto a cemetery. Dead flowers formed a skeleton army, in heaps with brown creases on them. In dreams they followed her like fire, turning flame to a stream of petals that wilted as they fell. The bleached membranes crumbled, wretched things; stems tumbled sluggishly into smeared piles. Torrid ash inscribed chalked streaks upon her, smelling of corpulent sweetness. And in escaping, having been here, she felt she broke off a piece of something, somewhere in herself.

She explored the center of the village. Despite constant wanderings, she hadn't been here in a very long time. An elderly man carried two pails of water, a smile on his face, a hat on his head. Three children ran in a circle, playing a game for which she had no name. Beside the road, inside dwellings arranged opposite each other, a multitude of mothers, fathers, sons, daughters, lovers, milled over wheat and grinding stone, already working on that night's dinner.

She sat on a bench again. Nearby, soon to be breached from the inside, stood the gates to a familiar temple. Everywhere whirled people and noise: shiftings from a shut door, the turning handle, boot-soles making footprints, shouts and cries of laughter. For a billion days, the street had been just like this: a million lifetimes.

She walked again, not towards her house yet but down a street she rarely traveled. A fence ran beside her, without moving. She passed three families going the other way. All she'd known for the greater period of her life, but she'd been *bigger* then, without confinement. But that gate didn't open for her anymore. Her universe was a closed off universe.

From a house, very far up ahead—a strangely proportioned house, a pale one, without open walls, nor even traces of a garden—her parents emerged. Both, like her, had darkish blond hair. Unlike her, they were red, and they sweated.

They held hands, father falling behind to be led.

Laura lunged into the bushes. Her father strutted, while her mother bustled, emphasizing hips. They wore the same clothes as the last time she'd seen them: a world apart.

Then they were gone, but another couple emerged, even happier looking than her own parents, except these belonged to Gidian. In like fashion, they bustled, until, having just passed her, they turned in her direction; walked past; opened a door in the closest house; and went inside.

There were no windows on the bottom floor of the house both parents had left originally, so she entered through the front door.

Inside, a hallway split, leading two places, leading nowhere. Smoky mist hung upon fibers, permeating essence over a sweaty undertone. The carpet had stains on it, none of them shaped like footprints. The walls barely stood. With everything in herself, Laura ate revulsion.

Her dress brushed lightly against her knees. She turned at a crossroad, and the smell got worse. She pinched her nose. From distant rooms, heavily muffled, came a sound like screaming, and hard, heavy thumps. In all her bad dreams she didn't think she could imagine something scarier.

Perception narrowed. The corridor became a singularity, tapestries slung all along its length.

She heard a swoosh. Turned.

Behind her stood a thin, sweaty, balding old man, his loose skin like a full-body wrinkle, hands extended to either side as he reached out to grab her. On his face he wore the strangest expression she'd ever seen. Everywhere else, he wore nothing at all.

Gidian fell out of his personal universe. Electricity wroth in place of his spine.

Banter had never been difficult for him, so he managed it, but the banter took place on a beam high, high in the sky. He never got past the suspicion that this couldn't be Laura, it was Sarah *pretending* to be Laura, to see if he'd recognize her. His head hurt.

The girl left him to a personalized hell. In it, reality had taken on the properties of a broken stick. For many hours he cried, looking at the wreckage of his instrument until darkness made it impossible; even then he imagined.

His hair was a mess. His skin felt like the mucky river, a polluted part where children void their bowels. His hat crumpled a few feet away. His skull throbbed when he touched it.

Sometime, he wasn't sure when, the light changed, but despite morning, he saw very little.

He gathered the wreck into his arms, a mess of strings and splinters, trashed pylons, deadened harmonics. Pieces stuck in his palms but he didn't notice till one jabbed in further. His eyes felt dry as dead rivers. His heart had fallen from his body.

Tenderly, like a child, he cradled his instrument. He stumbled in whatever direction. A piece fell and he picked it up carefully, dropping other pieces: a cycle. Autonomous moans. He tried to stop but he couldn't, taken over by his new self, the victim.

Twice he passed children. The first, screaming, ran from him. The second began crying and also ran, shouting for help. He barely noticed them, excluded as they were from his exiled universe. This new person, a fraction, had no constitution in self and body.

He arrived home to find the hill slanted just like he did. He'd kept his promise, he thought, but had found nothing worth returning to.

::::::::::::::::::

In Gidian's youth, brightness had constituted perception. Ever since he'd come into himself, into music, something must have taken its place. He thought himself charming with his long hair and thin body, but he never realized they didn't leave him alone out of courtesy. They avoided him.

At the very beginning, before the ritual, his best friend had been a girl named Sarah. They played children games for which he had no name. Her blond hair matched his, and they liked to imagine themselves brother and sister. When they were older they would get married.

He had no memory of it, nor of her. When the time came to become part of the ritual, she was the first thing he forgot. Most probably she'd forgotten him too—but had it been easy? He'd forgotten to care, as he forgot many things. He mattered in a way she never could, and someday he would discover music. The less real he became the further he fell, and farther, until his body, his soul, lie beyond even the most daring of scavengers.

He'd been so young he'd actually lost the memory, but its implications remained. It wrought a second self in him (the first), eradicating and replacing. Immediately, Sarah had come to him, but he didn't have time for her anymore. He walked proudly, purposefully, to a pulpit in the center of the village. He gathered his own crowd, and he wanted all their approval, their admiration.

Gradually he met two others: a little girl and an even littler boy. The girl had brown hair and prettiness, just like other girls in the village, but she glowed better because of herself. They'd gathered more than half the village to them. Gidian's own admirers dispersed into theirs. He felt an immediate surge of jealousy.

Later he thought himself too good for even this, but in newness he had no standards. He couldn't be a person in the casual sense. Jacob and Laura always handled it different. He always thought that meant they didn't understand what they had, but really he'd just been given too much.

:::::::::::::::::

More than likely, this tale bore some similarity to the past. Very little. Gidian had never placed much trust in memory, but nor had he any aversion to filling spaces. At any moment, in a timeless universe, an individual history can be erased, for never having existed at all. There might have been a little girl, but he doubted her name had been Sarah, and he doubted even more that she looked as he remembered her now—meaning she looked like Laura. Most probably he'd only garnered one or two stragglers. This past had drama, but that didn't make it true. It was just another story, he thought, and not a very good one.

:::::::::::::::::

In this void he'd created, nothing attached to form. His grief: entirely without object. In darkness, beneath the vague presence of a body, an immense well formed. Without space there could be no movement. He lost grasp of time gradually and without noticing. Light hung suspended; particle motion ceased. Solidarity—a lie of continuation. He cast it aside and the world became individual dots with no bonds between them. He'd seen the picture before by deconstructing the fabric, itself a unidimensional blanket. If he took effort, and gave force to motion, where did these fragments leave him? He couldn't imagine—the fuligan ache of a single soul trapped within the steal cold of heavy nonexistence, unable to breathe, unable to move, blood turned to vapor in his veins. Even the slightest motion might end the universe.

Suddenly formless, he discovered fear. Tiny orange specks, tiny green ones, sporadic in the rafters, the thin walls around him, the sodden floor below him. A sea of orange dots overwhelmed him, spreading into the landscape. Objects became rainbows. Fluxion constructs, mailable dimension—either it flooded him or he dispersed into it. If he moved, all of it would come unglued, but he was no longer capable. Awareness latched onto continent and landscape, those digits that before had been only one part of vision. He became stillness, encompassing all time, all distance. Light decried color, suspending waterfalls in highlight time. Eventually, or from the very beginning, he had renounced perception, encompassed into the unperception. Continually, perpetually he flooded, ceasing any recognizable sense; but he also relinquished sensation and feeling. He surged into himself, the globular dimension.

The first time he'd seen Sarah, not so long ago, he'd thought her beautiful. Without knowing, he might have loved her. Laura herself was too little for him, too real to encompass, but could he capture that? (if he could take that from her?) He found the means to create anew. Did he do her justice? She'd come from within herself, within others. All that exists diffuses; all that is created comes, in some way, from that which exists already. Without energy from the sun, he had no way of sustaining her, of sustaining himself. All that constitutes an individual he had given her. But where had he taken it from, and how long could he go on without it?

The first time he'd seen her, he'd spoken through her, to himself. His unconscious feared already at an inevitable need to fill. He'd come forward to himself, through her, and he'd asked, with Laura's voice, if she was real yet. Without mediums, even links splintered beneath the ground, she might die, and he might die, and their souls might disperse to cruel fountains. Fear took the place of grief; thought bonded to memory, to connections, to meaning. Existence reconstituted sense and implementing organ. Without his body he was blind, in all senses, just as others were blind to him.

He despised himself and his own mistakes, his blond hair, sense of misdirection. He was nothing but a dot in a prism of specks and rainbows. Even music was nothing but invisible. He asked questions to no one, and received no answer—at least, not emerging from within himself—but all things are transient. In all possibility, even from a paradox within it, he had experienced the entire life-cycle of the three dimensional universe… like it, taking place all in a single timeless moment.

In a distant corner where only the sun falls lie the remnants of an altar. It appears little but a lump packed together by time. It does not hint of holiness. Small stones litter its base; weeds wind into openings. Once this ground had known ceremony. Now, it knows only memory.

Families had gathered here to worship. Their clothes, despite rare materials (even then stitched out of a preexisting supply of cloth with only the threads grown on fibers) had been different, even if they were still clothes. During worship, chants they uttered. The priest led these services. He commanded great, great respect.

Even during casual times, children had played here. There had been a tree, and benches, and finer sand, and softer grass. Occasionally one might pray on their own. Incense they burned, spreading that same ceremonial dust. Afterwards they swept the holy ashes below, to enrich the earth.

Alters such as these became meaningless. The earth was not rich. Holiness is an aspect taking place entirely within the human element, which attaches itself at random to varying elements; it is ritual in tribute to symbols, but also a symbol itself. Like all things, symbols can be very easily forgotten.

::::::::::::::::::

Once, say the very oldest legends, there was a time when our people had wings.

For a moment Laura came detached from herself. She hung like a doll on a wire, with a geometric magnification of his face and many wrinkles. His swollen eyes, so close, so large, resembled explosions. He had warm, flabby fingers, garrulously smooth, so sweaty they stained her shoulders... and at any moment he might pounce, closing hands around her throat before crushing her with his filmy weight....

Reality lurched, taking on his lurid properties, swirled in his bagginess. Stumbling into a wall, she almost fell, whereat the swamp (yes, he was a swamp, grown over by moss, seeped in humidity) receded to a distant projection, that shifted as she ran. But something still felt wrong (*he* was wrong!), as though he'd never let go, and clung to part of her still, and if she turned, she would see her old self in suspended animation, his prisoner....

She lost her way, and found what she did at this place's mercy, suspecting it had none—seeing no one despite omnipresent moaning. Those moans might have been trapped here by time and repetition; or, more frightfully, might come from the building itself.

She discovered a stairway. Twice she tripped on the long hem of her dress. An overturned chair had broken the far wall, and grease stained the carpet. The window, thankfully, was open, and purity blew from it, to her, without smelling of sweat, and rot, and everything else within this place.

The height frightened her, and gave her nausea.

The window sill splintered beneath her fingers. The frame was small, but her body seemed to elongate like water, or slide like a petal: and she fell, quickly, heavily, like a rock dropped from near the middle of the body, and landed with a similar sound. Unlike a petal, her leg and arm absorbed the impact admirably (though not well), but like water she spread, become a skid mark on a big surface, her essence dispersed by flatness.

Vision swam, as did thought. She imagined the house reached for her. It had long crooked hands, and laughed like an old man, or a demon.

She ran.

A wall of bushes gave way into the clearing beyond, and she sat beneath the tree to nurse acquired wounds. She hadn't come here since the first time Gidian had called her “Sarah”. That seemed like a long time, but really it wasn't.

Still, something in her felt as if it had been tossed against a wall—but more than that, she hurt. One leg seemed alright, but the other, having taken the impact, didn't. Only one shoulder worked. She moved both and pretended not to cry. The pain made sure she did.

Her whole body was covered in sweat, and cool air chilled her suddenly. She didn't like feeling she'd taken some part of that place with her. Crying made her feel weak, too delicate for the real world. That made her cry harder.

Maybe she fell asleep, but it seemed like when the sweat dried, a solar globe took formation: a crimson orb above her, around her, magnifying the heat to purify. But it failed, and she had never been pure: though her hair and skin caught fire, lifting wildly within tongues of flame, her soul melting in the inferno. Maybe afterwards she would be reborn (yes, golden light in the midst of swirling ashes, her limbs shining with it, aglow), but she didn't know. Was there anything to run from? But more importantly: anywhere to run *to*?

Helping herself with a stick, she found the river, where she bathed. She hadn't done so in many days, but normally the garden kept her clean by association. Grit came off in flowing water, as did many other things invisible, that had been lodged within her, and downstream, as the current knifed upwards, a purifying mechanism took effect, filtering silt by gravity.

Had she seen this water before? The river, despite being within her, within the valley, bore no singular properties. Within it were infinite drops of water; then the drops within droplets. If she filled a container, she ignited invisible transformation.

And what then?

There was no singular flow, but there seemed to be: bound by direction, separate in element. She stood naked to dry. Her skin shone very beautiful; the gentle slopes of it, the silken grades. For the first time in this life, she remembered what it meant to be a woman. But she had no answers to her questions, and no one to ask but herself. Questions about life and maturity had never occurred in any quantifiable sense, not in relevance to everything else. Too long her life had been a chronicle of the relevant object, that left no place for her within it.

::::::::::::::::::::::

The day she found her new self (and lost the old), she'd been in her garden. Even so young she already had one.

An invisible call rang out, or message, she didn't know what to call it, except that she knew she'd be taking part in the ritual now, that she'd become the ritual, and it made her exceptional. The sun came closer, as though with uplifted hands she might caress it immaterial. But an evil flower bloomed within her, feeding on oily liquid, to bask in rapturous light. In many ways that oily liquid was the presence of the sun, as it took the place of her true self.

She went toward that call. But though she heard much, it was distant, without direction. Her parents weren't there, and she didn't have a sister yet, or she didn't think so. Every house was empty, and no one came to her. Down pathways she heard many voices, but not the ones she needed.

Only long after did someone come for her, a much younger man she didn't recognize. He took her hand and led her to the center of the village, where she found a small crowd and two boys. She laughed, because seeing them made her happy. There had been more people before, the blond one explained meanly, but they'd gotten tired of waiting. The other boy didn't have anything to say at all, just stared at her.

That night, as she slept, strange thoughts came to her, strangest among them that tomorrow she had something to wake up for.

Linear time began for her then. In its presence bloomed only that one dark flower.

::::::::::::::::::::

The sun wiped her dry, even if she didn't move for long after that. Returning to her dress, she wondered if Jacob had really stared at her. Very possibly she'd gotten there first, and only been afraid of getting lost. She could only guess at having been in the garden; felt very lost without knowing if it mattered.

She came to the wastelands: all paths lead to them. Within the walls sang many souls, the tortured theme of eons. Turquoise spears tore brigantine clusters, shredding huge gray chunks. Blistered sand tumbled at strange angles. Burgundy stretched within metamorphic carnage: womb and living tissue.

Rediscovering her own intentions, she found Gidian's cottage. Grass withered around it. The tree had fallen to pieces. Formless stuff came from within, an inky black she recognized. She approached slowly, without fear. The soil she strode upon: like stone. Smell of cinders and decimation.

Inside, she saw Gidian naked. His pale skin played host to soupy darkness, wafting occasionally to mist. Much of his hair had burned. She heard sounds, but not necessarily of consciousness, nor humanity. Occasionally he quivered. A hole had been blast into the far wall; light slipped through to be fed upon. Gidian rest upon dirt in the place of remembered floorboards. Some time into her vigil, he began muttering. He clutched something tightly against his chest. Weak limbs gave little protection.

No humor remained from their last meeting. She did not throw a stone. Gradually he stirred, then moaned—alien tones only *borrowing* his voice. He sat weakly, without noticing her. Thin bones shuffled, caging weak organs. His eyes shone a pale color for which she had no name.

"Sarah?" His voice came ever weaker, yet free of evil tones. She stared at him for many moments without answering.

Later, she didn't even know if she'd given one.

::::::::::::::::::::

When a tree sprouts, reaching fingers break from within kinetic podshells, sculpting atoms to make the extension. Cumulative bloom becomes lightning; grasping spines, refine curvature. Many roots sink on an aqueous pilgrimage. Growth takes off in opposing directions, exponentiating upon the original object. Diffusing presence potentiates invisible motion, whereby space becomes holographed in trajectory, shadowing bright red lines.

::::::::::::::::::::

Laura pretended she didn't need a cane, but walking had lost all sense of symmetry. The unity of body and motion was much too elaborate, and came across too smoothly. Only now did she understand why the body had two sides, and why they matched.

She sat in the market. It wasn't a market in any accurate sense, but instead a place to trade and gossip—mostly gossip. She counted five stalls, two selling more than one item, one not selling an item at all. Finely polished stones, carved (surely after much effort) into cylinders, hung on twines of the stringy vine used to sow clothes. Ruddy scenery made smears across sheets of bound lining—thin, woody stuff from the stem of a rare tall plant—upon which one might impress a variety of images, mostly pictures of the walls, sun, villagers and familiar locations, though occasionally the artist drew certain well-considered images from his own imagination after patterning them according to familiar local. Next to them stood a tall, strong man (who Laura noticed had no hair on his torso or beneath his arms; he wore no shirt, apparently flaunting this) who might perform various manual labors—he had no wife, and was reputedly an extremely poor cook.

An old woman told stories to young children—Laura didn't know if she were a member of the marketplace or not. A group spoke loudly, and giggled often. An impatient boy performed acrobatics as he waited for his mother. Two little girls (though they were really very close to her own age) sang an unfamiliar song. The older women huddled together, centerpiece to this nexus of experience. Her own mother, Laura thought, might easily fit among them.

The sellers she knew; the mothers, the children—but though on some level she recognized them, by some cosmic accident either they or she had come disconnected from name. In their place were only the shadows of symbols: from gap, to gap, to gap. Space wavered around them, or within her. Thought became blindness in the semantic deficiency.

If she wanted, she thought, she could get a necklace or a bracelet, then she could wear them, so that when people saw her they really saw jewelry. Or she could get a picture of herself, and carry it, so people seeing her would really see mashed jelly pigments. Or she could get that man to make improvements on Gidian's house, so after they got married they could live there forever like they planned—though that wasn't a very good idea, because she hadn't been making plans. When she went home tonight she would show everyone what she'd bought, or she'd show them herself, and they might find that entertaining before they asked about her leg. After that Michelle might laugh, and her parents voices might get high and self-righteous—that is, if she found them there. If not, she would sit either with or without Michelle, then when Michelle got there they would talk about themselves, and Michelle's friends who she didn't care about. But worse, if she saw her parents, could she still think of them as themselves? When she went home they would light a fire till morning. Tomorrow she would tell Gidian she loved him—she didn't, but when she picked her love up it had two sides, and all she had to do was turn it around—and give a friend a flower. That would make happiness for her. That would restore her again. Then she would swim naked like a petal drifting downstream. She could still do that when she felt like a little girl.

She stood, still needed a cane, and bought a single stone in exchange for that flower she would grow tomorrow. Tonight she would look at it to see streaks of frost curving into the blue. There were no secrets there, but there were no secrets anywhere. Her world, as it existed now, was the best and most well kept secret but who's laughing? No one laughed at secrets anymore.

:::::::::::::::::::

As she turned to leave, a red-faced boy ran into the market: runner of marathons. Conversations stopped. Expectation built up as he bent over. Sand stuck between his toes. His neck shone very bronze.

"It's Jacob," he said. "He came back!"

Gidian lacked the strength to move. He shifted shape: a reintroduction to perspective. Cold mud (dirt mixed into sweat) covered half of him. His head hurt. So did his back. Blood circulated slowly; limbs burst into iced needles. His torso had frozen, because he wore no shirt, and his toes would never move again. He ran a hand along one arm until he realized he felt it.

He fell three times. The third he stumbled into a wall, and brought part of it with him. The floor disappeared. He searched for a doorway, but left through the hole in the wall—climbing awkwardly, accidentally hurting himself: a carapace of scars.

Outside he saw no light, but he heard a low-rumble; felt he'd stumbled into another room, identical to the first. Nothing moved—intrusion onto his ethereal sense. He touched his new gouges; explored old ones: imagining himself some torrid monster, all gaping open and splintered. He sat back into the grass. Thin grass, and dirt below it. Logic told him he'd fallen outside. That distant rumble he recognized: the walls. Very often one overlooks the familiar.

He rose slowly but without falling; wanted badly to be clean. There must be clothes somewhere (he'd tossed them carelessly as he worked, never caring to pick them up). Finding none, he put the walls at his back and turned to where he thought the path might be—where it wasn't—wondering then at the similarities between vision and blindness: differential applications. He saw no sun, so either it was night, or he had gone blind. He doubted both, but only the second seemed possible. Within him, at the realization, something began to topple, teetering towards fear.

But instead he chose denial.

For the first time in days he began to sing: immersion within this appalling construct. He stepped carefully, but every step felt familiar. Music reminded him of reality here, the solidity beyond veils—and when he looked past it, he could see....

Like shadows, faint outlines ran in darkness; ran everywhere, a quick sketch over thinning objects. He saw every blade of grass as a single spear; tall stalked plants in a cylindrical spiked forest. Layer built on layer. After it outlined the immediate, he saw further (shape rushed backwards like wind) until the web turned into all he could see, a thin green multitude, perimeters overlapping. Overlap encompassed the visual.

Light broke on the tapestry—but not light in any familiar sense. Metallic purples fell onto hanging leaves, the closed buds; swirled in dirty green; washed with bursts of clear, painful white. The light hurt his eyes, but he saw. An anti-light. Everything within it, all properties. And when he looked into the sky, he saw an anti-sun: perfect blackness hallowed to equal any fullness he knew.

He followed the shimmering pathway—it shifted—to the flaming river, where he bathed in fractals.

::::::::::::::::::

At the absence of a secondary star (it shrank, and finally disappeared), Gidian's world transgressed in darkness. The temperature chilled, and nameless elements bombarded him, the river trickling softly. He imagined colossi at war. He imagined cosmic exchange.

But nothing moved, and all was silent.

::::::::::::::::::

A golden needle drove into the empty sky, igniting bands like a vibrant star. Those bands subdivided, making more bands, and new tones slipped between. Nebulous, possessing arms like a spiral, the star appeared to fluctuate, gaining fullness until taking on cardinal proportions. White needles ignited patterned layers, and beyond these spread a sequence of ripples. The white grew longer, and wider. Empty blue developed at the edge as golden hues returned, blossomed to a tapered oval. This melded through the white, narrowing as its heated center returned, primarily gold, and much smaller.

Slowly, still tapering into the same horizontal eye, the sun began to get larger.

::::::::::::::::::

Gidian returned home, where he clothed himself, but set off immediately. His second pair of boots weren't as nice as his first (apparently lost), but he wore them. Quite on purpose he spurned his final remaining hat.

Later, when he saw his reflection, which didn't show in the river at night, he found he'd lost most of his hair. What remained was barely longer than Jacob's had been, and he would have to cut off more because of the sizzled ends. That hair had been with him since the first time he'd gone to the hill. He supposed it was right that it go, even if he did miss it.

Walking slowly, and pausing on occasion to sniff, he hunted. Trails ran everywhere, intersecting. Utilizing combined senses, he followed: now through gaps, now between houses, then a hundred feet in the air. His nostrils tensed. Thighs began to twitch. On and off, he developed an erection.

His prey would be there. He had prey. It was quiet, and brown, and subtle, and sexual, and opulent, and inquisitive, and fay, and he would find it. Nor would it run. Nubile arches instigated tornadoes. Its scent—scentless—nosed between leaves. The flavor caressed him in taste places. Only when he reached out to touch it, it hadn't come.

He found himself in a clearing he'd never seen. In all aspects it was absolutely insignificant. The ground resembled any other ground—flat, yet occasionally lumpy—and sand showed in it, but no footprints. On the other side, barely, he made out a lump of stones, significantly crumbled, vine-shot impregnating them.

Two paths led in one direction each. Down one he would find the thing he wanted. Regardless of decision, and what that decision meant, he would still be making a decision. No, but he couldn't. Turning around, he retraced the last turn he'd made, where he finally decided.

Along the way he met three children. And spoke to none. Village custom called for a greeting, which he might turn to after the destruction of so many previous selves, but he would turn preceding the hunt. If it had an afterwards. It had never been his custom, but until now he'd never realized he had one.

Three reeds masked two children, the second and third. They rubbed, and kissed, and giggled. He'd seen them before, yet never together. Also, he'd walked here many times before, and never seen the two *here*. That meant they were new—or if not new, they represented new permutations.

When he passed, they became history.

He closed in on his victim. He found another clearing with a rock and a tree. The tree daggered into sunlight; the rock bled surface shadows. He'd come here twice already, but only now did it begin to matter. During his life he'd come here more times than he could count. It was a convenient place to hide.

Falling to his knees, he began digging. Pared layers slid between fingers, into fingernails. Handfuls hit the bushes. Sweat rolled down his forehead; sunk in a whirling ocean. Later, when he'd finished (a tunnel, or a hole), he would wash his hands in the river, for filtering vessels to relocate.

As he dug, he imaged a gigantic doorway. The door shone bronze, or brass, or gold, without understanding colors he couldn't know. In the handles glittered beautiful stones, twin insignia, one in the center of each door—but no, up close they were different.

As they swung open (a gradual, loping motion, flirting with forever) gold light blessed the flooring, and gave him benediction: a maverick illumination, piercing his eyes. The deeper he went, the light became brighter, and stronger. Not strength as in brightness, but an actual muscularity of substance, a power. Brighter and stronger.

Behind them he saw the an array of white dots, a mandala—

But no, it was too bright to see.

::::::::::::::::::::

Gidian imagined his monster as a purple troll so much larger than him that he could barely compete with its big toe. Way in the stratosphere, within one nostril, it wore a thick metal band. Huge teeth smacked in leathery gums. He knew, even without prior experience, that its breath didn't smell very good.

::::::::::::::::::::

The branch broke after years of dead hanging. It fell quickly, and landed with the sound of crisping leaves.

::::::::::::::::::::

Gidian sighed and looked upwards at the sun. This new hill resembled his old one, but not quite. Gentle gravity dumped its weight on him, meaning he'd gotten lucky. From up high gravity didn't tend to be so gentle.

But there was something wrong.

Maybe he imagined it, but it looked as though the sun were getting bigger.

III

A crowd had gathered around Jacob—more people than Laura had ever seen in the same place at once. Most came as families, proud father expelling his chest, dragging the frantic mother, holding their confused children between them. They formed an uproarious static cloud, where words weren't.

Laura searched for her own family. Twice she found them, before realizing the little girl she saw wasn't her, nor even her replacement. By virtue of her immersion, one person began to resemble another, until she saw one person as all persons, everyone. She forgot not only who she was looking for, but, more importantly, why she wanted to find them; and having lost that, she pretended something of herself hadn't gone with it, like a flier from dreams—but something surely had.

She drifted to the front of the crowd, pushing shyly. Her temples throbbed. Nothing in life had prepared her for this (not open spaces, long days, shorter nights, heavy thought, warm mornings, or any combination of those things), and consciousness spun within a scary, scary nebula, as though she had never lived at all... and in a sense, that part of her would stay here forever.

The crowd had become the village. Those arriving now were stragglers who hadn't been at home when the message came. They were more confused than most, and most were very confused indeed. They gave her pressure.

Jacob stood with his father in the center of this glandular organism. The old man shriveled beneath his cloak, bearing loose skin and hanging eyes. Rotted colors showed in his cheeks, beneath copious sweat, before multitudinous expression. But Jacob himself looked much as she remembered, excepting only the color of his skin: bleach white, as though a succubus had feasted on the pigments within it, or he'd been duplicated and pasted through dimension. She remembered his clothes—a brown vest over faded pants, much too small but not as tattered as one would expect considering they'd belonged to the old man before, and been worn throughout a journey.

Arrivals slowed until there was no one left to come. Conversation fell beneath an immense pillow. Much speculation took place in the smoke they created; like ghosts, they hung on that blank face before them. Gidian's parents emerged, as they were often wont to do, and calmed the crowd, despite silence. Someone coughed. The mother ran two hands through her hair.

Her speech was too painful to mention. Within it, she introduced Jacob, whom all knew, and gave him welcome. She told him how much he'd been missed, but lied, because he hadn't been missed at all. Afterwards, she cleared her throat as if to speak again; began to do so; thought better of it; and fell quiet.

Jacob spat oblivion. His eyes had dilated to the point they were without color, and strayed lazily—Laura couldn't tell if he was just without interest, or if there was nothing left to see. A murmur arose. It grew gradually louder, a barrage of questions Jacob ignored, in voices that grew increasingly frustrated.

Then, when frustration became resentment, they began to leave.

The priest led Jacob away. He followed apparently without notice, his eyes—weak blips on feeble cords—traveling from nothing, to nothing, to nothing. Seen from a different angle, he was extraordinarily thin: a hole. The crowd left also, and what remained held nothing visible, but beyond the physical hung the remnants of their aura, that must be imagined to be perceived. Laura felt imprisoned within fictitious amber, thinking that maybe if she didn't move, think, live, they might return, or Jacob might return, and everything would be right again. But of course it wouldn't.

She left with a new hole in herself. That hole had been dug by an inevitable feeling of betrayal, and she blamed it all on Jacob: that he could come back, that he could be here, with nothing to say. She couldn't believe him.

She chose the path to his house. It was the first time she'd done so since his departure, though she'd considered it many times. Even in Jacob's absence it had seemed she might find him there; at least a folded up, inanimate, two dimensional version. She didn't know what she wanted from him, but she had to get something.

The walls grew larger as she approached. Jacob lived on the outskirts of the village, but not so far as to be a part of the wastelands, because no one could live there, except Gidian, and he'd been insane since the beginning of this life. On the occasions she'd visited, the house seemed broken, useless. It had only one window, thick dark walls, and a big, big door.

She knocked tentatively, which hurt her hand, and a kind of fear caught up with her—a fear she had forgotten so long ago, when she'd come here to help Jacob, instead of find him. She brushed the hair from her face, attempting to smooth her dress, but accomplished very little.

She heard footsteps so heavy she *felt* them approaching. They opened the door. Jacob's father was not happy to see her.

"Hello," she said—and wasn't sure she'd survive.

Gradually, with much insistence, she made her way inside. The priest shut the door—he hated her, everyone else but her more than anyone—and pointed to the table. On it, Jacob's hands formed a cross, and he sat abnormally straight. She approached, but he never even looked her way.

"Jacob?" she asked. "Are you there?"

He barely turned, presenting wide, dark eyes. The more she said, the less he paid attention. She had so many questions—questions about life and place and things he'd seen but most of all questions about herself, questions even he wouldn't be able to answer—but no place to ask them, not in this apathy he gave. He blinked once, but not for her. She imagined he flared his nostrils.

"Alright," she said. "Be like that."

Up close his face grew unnaturally smooth, as though somewhere his skin had been removed, or cut into pieces, or he'd been burned, only to be replaced later. Inside he was a fiery outcrop where no forests bloomed, and lonely wanderers feared to camp. Icy cliffs struck where the acid didn't flow; granite rain turned the earth to beaten powder.

She spoke, but her speech shot through huge caverns without echoing: and if he heard her at all (either inside or outside his shriveled self; this body if it did constitute self) time-dark and distance turned language to long cool rock-whispers that came, that ebbed without sound; his mind a truth entombed under a cold garden on a freezing planet, where the flowers grew inky and black. Those flowers clustered above his grave, shivering softly in ice crusted petals, beneath a chilled purple sun.

She left him there. He'd come back without answers, having lost not only questions, but also himself. What little she remembered (what little she imagined): his eyes, his cold skin, his vacant mind. She'd been right, and he'd been right, and everything in the world was nothing but crazy.

The priest shut the door at her back, marking transition: boldness and breadth (he hated her). Dim light fell into a bar at her feet, and she stepped over it, resolved that she would never come again, that Jacob had nothing and more nothing to give her, this daemon prophet from an abscess beneath the universe. The distance of him, void of human warmth, connection to the sun, had no place in her material universe, the plane of hard shapes and quiet moments, soft life and warm memories. He replaced the void he left, but filled it in negative, canceling space. His heart and hands and homunculi bearing.

She pulled a string from around her neck, the single bead she'd purchased earlier, a dark red distilled from some unknown flower. That flower had died to make this rock, or reshape it. Did it comfort her to know life went somewhere else? (if it did?) Someday she would grow old and older until she died, and then she would go somewhere, even if she didn't know where—or she would, if she was here at all. She could become a rock, or a flower, or a blade of grass, or a kind of motion in the walls, or she could live in the sun, churning in energy, until the day spat her out again, and she could be herself in a burning meteor.

Along the way she met a girl she knew, even if she didn't know her right now. The girl had dark brown hair and wore a blue dress. They stopped and talked for a while. Laura gave her the stone, or the necklace, or the necklace with the stone on it, because she didn't need it to be looked at anymore—she hadn't ever.

"Have you talked to Jacob?" the girl asked. "After the assembly?"

"No," Laura said. "I haven't seen him at all."

::::::::::::::::::::

A fireball shot of the walls and exploded, streaming backwards into a fountain. Treacle gush and the hard-cool dry, turning silt to diamonds as grass blades bowed. Mountains came to life and suffered instantaneous erosion; wilted peaks shallow as a young girl's breast. The torso stretched.

Rapid energy raced within them, cycling, cyphering. Near the bottom their shape stayed smooth or rocky, but higher up furious change took effect. They were almost difficult to look at. The monstrous churn discarded shape, size, and color, replacing them with beautiful warfare. Normally these days came rarely, and the walls shifted in gradual, lethargic steps, like a giant at sleep. Recently they'd come more often.

She put her hands on her hips. With the sun setting as it did, from behind someone might find her quite attractive: fine frame against thin cloth, bare limbs ashine, hair in a whirlwind, hips and thighs her feminine secrecy. She ground her foot, scraping stray pebbles. One she threw into the furious light at the rim of the world, watching it pierce that light... a heavy bounce and roll. She breathed deeply, squinting into distant bright.

Without fear, she retrieved that rock (she had to go all the way to the base, something many boys did only on the most voracious dares) before returning to her route. She carried it for many steps before tossing it again, this time without hitting anything. It spun unevenly.

She skipped, racing darkness. Strange mirror devices forced time backwards, sky gone dim dark orange, path alight with flame from mirrors. But soon, very suddenly, even that was gone. Exponential time thrust her into the past creation.

She continued past a broad face, upon which might be carved the phoenix. Muted rumbling her sound and tracking. She slowed, measuring footsteps, scanning dim cracks. Dusk had taken joy with it, release had fallen, but through it all, the many stages, she was still here.

She discovered the cave. It had waited for her, or it hadn't. No fear sprung up in her, but problems of pacing berated. When she'd come close enough, the feeling of relocation, of crushing, of rebirth; there and prominent, genuflecting spawn in her parenthetic core.

“Yeah,” she said. “I knew it.”

Sunshine in the Valley

For a long time Gidian became a sphere curling in on itself, crying deeply—all a tingling spread through extremities, an excitement. His clothes bore traces of dirt, next to the hole he'd created. Within it he'd become a meteor.

Replenishing the earth, he wondered how much of his life had been spent walking, ruling out the portion spent playing music. He swung his arms and blood clotted in the tips of his fingers, subtly dispersing presence.

Beginning that new tradition, when he passed someone he offered to sing them a song. All accepted in a similar manner, hesitant but with expectation. Their expression caused wonderment in him, at who he was, at who he he'd been, and what his past selves had done in this singular life.

Each time he sang the same song, the only song worth remembering. No—every time he sang it different, but it had the same structure, even if it didn't have the same words, or the same meaning. At least they seemed to like it: shy rush, turn and pull, wind of flicker, rupture remaking, figurine ghost the flame of a candle

He spent hours walking, adding to previously mentioned ratios, and went many places (an old tree where he'd taken many girls, a solemn place where an offshoot of the river trickled into a pond, a cabin), sky seeping to the early gradients of evening, gentle gold brokering fine mist across he and his eventually darkening world.

Later he stumbled into a funeral-gate of flowers, spilling cannibalized to the one true surface. Singing fates proclaimed deathly curvature, defiling, regurgitated. His signs and directions (the mind and the way) abandoned shells as the spirits thanked them thoughtfully. Yes, and where did he follow the spirits? (to a grove on the far side of vacant planets, to a city of rustwires and the caw of imaginary creatures?) Diagonal pacing inverted into an idiot semblance, dissolving mind-sight and hurry, breaking the prominent fixture. Pyres rustled; whispering.

Ahead, behind a curtain of flowers, something shivered. Dry rasp and febrile slurping. Gidian hesitated. That thing was a monster that ate flowers, red skinned and many spined, face and fangs, scale and fiber, its breath like steaming acid. Inside he created it, building from the skeleton but replacing bones, lengthening angles to heighten the incision.

Fear spread like water—or its physical manifestation. He wasn't sure it had come to his head yet, that it would ever come. Cool falls trickled syrupy in his torso, spiring in a gale; stopping to turn valves, to spread him open. Sudden rush and his bowels retracted. Forehead quivered and he passed through a glistening tunnel, color pasted across its deep sliding body.

Something rustled and he saw it again... this time as the hint of a rustling, linked just as skull, arms, crossfire, feasting on flowers, a hunger to last ten million lifetimes; universe burst into a flurry of descending petals, chauffeur currents into the storm beyond dreamscapes....

He borrowed a knife instead of stealing one, and went to the river to cut his hair. He thought of shaving it all, but only briefly. He hadn't known the man, but the man had known Gidian's name, so he felt entitled to asking permission. No one trusted him, but he knew how to be persuasive.

The knife was long, thin, and sharp. Twice he cut himself, but he still possessed all his fingers. Probably the remnants would stay here for a very long time unless someone decided they wanted them—not likely.

Returning the knife, Gidian sang the man's family a song. All looked at him strangely upon seeing the other item he carried, just as the children on the path had done, but he had no trouble ignoring that. He finished. They clapped and proclaimed him a prodigy, even if he'd gotten too old for that now, and he felt important.

He stayed to eat dinner with them. The man's wife had been dead for years; she wasn't herself anymore; she was gone. He used this as his primary conversation piece, merging casual information, such as his cooking abilities, with tragic lifestyle reflections, such as the difficulty of caring for two children, both present. He doted on Gidian increasingly, a fatherly gesture to which Gidian had become unaccustomed. This was the first time in a long time he'd eaten with anyone willingly, and he didn't have any sense of the conversational rhetoric, as this man revisited his own, replacing and relating. It was also the first time Gidian had cared to learn a name.

The kitchen resembled many, if not all kitchens Gidian had seen. This did not, and had never surprised him. The walls were a grainy brown. Four chairs maintained their accustomed places at the table, as though they'd always been there, and never been moved. Everyone made efforts to eat silently.

Gidian found the children nice enough, and discovered during the meal that they were twins, a boy and a girl, even if they didn't look it. They peaked at him out of the corner of their eyes, conversing excitedly between themselves.

Finally, despite a firm look from their father, the boy asked,

"Did you see him?"

"Who?"

"Jacob," the girl said. "He came back."

"He did?" Gidian paused, spearing his plate. "That's nice."

But could he dismiss it, and what was he dismissing? He with both hands in his pockets, thinking of Jacob—pretending not to think of him, for the implications he had.

He returned home for the first time in days. But despite what he'd done, where he'd been, he hadn't really been gone so long, and in many cases he'd been gone longer.

He hadn't been defeated, but something felt different. Inside, despite so many different layers, he was still the same person, Original Self, but it had been thrown against walls, bisected, distorted. He didn't have the strength for that anymore, or the willingness to fight. Dedication to symbols, to effort and love: they stripped him of himself, replacing that with a profane willingness to *just be*. So now he ate lunch with villagers, and asked before borrowing things.

At home he threw himself onto a comfortable surface. He had a dream about himself, like most of his dreams. In it, he wore brown cape and big tall hat, his least favorite, and his hair was long again. Viewing from a point outside his body, he walked along the edge of a rocky crevice. Green flatness overtook him from behind, punctuated by rare objects. Wind blew his turban and his hair.

He trudged until slowing to remove a small object from his pocket. That object was a stone too insignificant to crumble, and he threw it into the hole. Moments later he paused again, throwing a dirty piece of metal. Next he tossed a dusty bottle. Then he removed his cloak, folds rippling as it flew, and his headdress joined it in a great twin spiral.

In one hand, previously hidden by the coat, an object shone too bright to see. This he carried for many moments until stopping to dangle it with one arm out over the gorge, torso swinging in its direction, pale mane lofted in a gale… and Gidian realized he *couldn't* let himself drop it; that object might be his heart, or his soul; but he couldn't stop himself because he wasn't himself—and the shining object began to fall, fell, and was gone.

Waking, it was obvious where he'd been (on the edge of the valley), but he wondered longer at who he'd become, and who he'd been watching; not because he didn't have an answer, but to defend what little of himself remained. How much else had Jacob taken from him, after strength, after reason, after beauty, and now identity too?

Dull stains overtook the window, crawling as the life drew within him. New weakness impregnated the wastes of creation.

He suffered.

Suddenly, and for the first time ever, he missed Laura. He hadn't spoken cordially to her for days, maybe never. More and more she'd become only a shadow of her daughter, whom he loved. He told himself he couldn't let that bleed into her, but without his knowing, it seemed to.

He set out for her house before remembering he didn't know where it was, but found it by luck regardless—or he called it that, afraid to acknowledge other implications for fear he might have permanently damaged her, have damaged them, by borrowing everything without asking.

He knocked on the door. Nothing moved, no action, so he went inside, where he found Laura's sister, an attractive girl with long brown hair, possibly more attractive than her sister when she wasn't asleep in a tangle of herself. Seeing her, he became horribly embarrassed; each step echoed loudly. Her lashes fluttered.

"Is Laura here?" he asked.

"She's been gone since last night," Michelle said. After telling him to leave—though to come back later, if he wanted to—she fell asleep immediately, and he returned to the morning wondering not so much why he felt incomplete (he did), but more than anything at what exactly he'd lost.

Jacob tumbled to the rocks, departing soul flung deep below. There he hung suspended, naked in thin silvery hands within a pocket of gray darkness. But it must have been a dream, or it felt like one, because he watched from outside himself, calmly as he floated on a second, silent pedestal.

He woke after another fall, back into himself this time, eating dirt, regurgitating euphoria. Solidity barricaded spirit, afloat in an ocean of gravity. Huge distance in his eyes, within them: dust and grasses before a thin banded horizon, entire worlds between it and he. These contained narrow objects, their size decreasing as distance did the opposite. Color bled from them, taking strength from contrast, uniqueness from infrequency.

The longer he looked, the smaller he felt; desisting from travel, a journey to nonexistent mind. Within him, a furnace threatened to burst, exploding hands, face, chest and body, melting bones. He walked, studying the ground at his feet, and like this he circled the valley—ashamed at his fear, swallowing cold acid in unbearable maintenance; going slowly to avoid breaching the perimeter, his entry-point in this world.

Where it entered the valley, Jacob came upon the river. It flowed over the walls, or slipped backward. He turned against the current, struggling against it; against himself. That tension took on many shapes, becoming a serpent as coils meshed web, solidifying to a glacier. In defiance, corrosion melted the glacier. Melt-off created an ocean, gigantic and cold. Currents broke out, stirring the winds above it.

Hurricanes flung harshness, slicing white mountains. Then the ocean evaporated, calming as it lost its very core. From beneath it rose a hot flaming sun.

Jacob lifted his eyes and ran. Seeing the horizon, he felt to justify it, himself, he must crush it all in a grasp of arms; but he didn't have the reach, no he didn't have the reach... and looked behind only when he'd gone far enough to escape seeing the valley, the sun. The land behind him spread identical to the land before: meaning he saw nothing.

He collapsed, and madness elapsed slowly. But somewhere he'd come temporarily to love it, his only companion in a big, big world.

The ground was very hard.

::::::::::::::::::::

Returning to the river required longer than expected, but he rediscovered his course. Something heavy rode on top of him, borne by a previously unused section of himself. The weight of deep earth. Of sinking.

The long green horizon measured an infinite circle, disappearing when he turned. As even this grew acceptable, he focused primarily on discrepancies in nearer terrain, containing details. On occasion, rocks might pierce the flatness, but none resembled those in the valley. He stayed along the river, with a casual inclination to wander. In the bank, where it had one, he searched casually, then more curiously, for signs of presence, but found none.

The need to survive had been bred out of his people by a trillion days in the underworld. Instead, and more urgently, he pondered his purpose here, whatever purpose he might have. The only thing that occurred to him was something to prove that it wasn't empty.

Sections of the sky dimmed, but only sections, as though far away multitudinous suns ebbed slowly, or imitations like the one's that used to be in lamps. And darkness fell, or an imitator of darkness, but it seemed other among those unseen same came alight—though not as many of them, mostly further in the distance—so even if he stood in a dark area, still alien blue kept light in it.

An eternity passed and he fell into another, dreaming of descent into a nebulous purple galaxy, holding arms and legs to himself, his tail cutting kaleidoscope stars, dots and dots in a geyser of dots. Vision blurred melting flames.

The fright and wind of it. A cocoon kept him safe amidst this cacophonous flurry. Momentum dulled his willingness to move.

He burst through cloud boundaries, rupturing stars, riding explosion. Crystal disintegration culminated to a slurry of pellets. Equilibrium replenished him, channeled from whatever place. He imagined the inside of the sun, or the center of the universe, but it couldn't be either. Neon shining ribbons fell languid into the cosmic river, replacing maelstrom descent.

Tranquility banished his sense of direction, replacing it with buoyancy, and soon he appeared recreated within a single bubble: gel-soft, languidly extending. The bubble dissipated and he filled with water. Distance took on indicators of shadow. A gigantic mouth opened within it. Proximity magnified proportion. It dwarfed him, the decks singed, its rigging discordant. Or maybe it was the silhouette of some gigantic beast, the kind known only in stories.

He awoke into brightness unfamiliar for lack of gold tones. His muscles ached from the walking he'd done, and would do the same in the nights to come. He drank from the river. His mouth had been dry but not thirsty, inducing paradox. Feeling hunger, though he knew it would do little without the sun, he removed his clothes and walked naked, drinking shallow nourishment. Without them, the air grew startlingly chilled. Redressing, he chewed on bitter grasses, but spat most, and swallowed little.

He slept without waiting for dusk. The bright air grew cold, grew thinner. He ached, groaned upon waking into this ache, and rolled continually from position, to position, to position. By opening his eyes, he would again acknowledge his presence in this place—and refused to do so. He did not dream, but imagined sensation, a barrage in windy darkness.

His resolve failed, and he found the sky still bright. He clung to it pitifully, with no way to separate the single days, the proceeding nights. Later, he confirmed the irregularity of these periods. When one side of the sky remained alight, some glow persisted. An approximate day might last half that time or forever. When he slept, who said he hadn't discarded eternity?

Sleeping a third time (he resolved at least to count how often he slept) he began walking further and further from the river, soon going out of its sight entirely. Yet he always returned there to sleep. In the mornings, or when he awoke, the water flowed painfully cold, icing in his stomach. Successive rests and he woke colder, curled tighter, but felt ever less.

Short grasses in an endless field, interspersed with pale bushes and patches of stones. These paled with progression, but he attributed it to his imagination. He saw tall rocks on the horizon, even mountains, but they disappeared as he slept or between departures in attention. What formations he reached tended to tapering cones, of sand or stone, that he touched without feeling, and never saw coming. Objects accumulated rarely, though twice he'd seen pairs of boulders, one even big enough to sit on, and once more a scattering of bushes.

Of trees, he witnessed even fewer. He'd been used to them in the valley, and admired them for being made of the toughest substance next to rock. On each he thought to carve his name before he realized he possessed no means to do it. There would be no one to read, either.

Cold pierced his bones, and he lost track of days. Grown delirious, he imagined it wasn't the landscape that grew colder but he; that, timeless, without sensation, the frost came from within him, regardless of the scenery or in reaction to it or neither. He wandered further from the river; ceased returning. Frequently he thought of it as having frozen. Sometimes he slept in the same area without taking a single step, or if he did he didn't know it—waking either backwards or forwards in time, shooting in dimension.

He would never find another sun, another valley. Either they were too far away or he wasn't meant to go there, and he imagined them cold, colder, bathed in this foreign light that froze him. How could there be light ahead of him, beside him? Their shadows fizzled definition; reflected. Different, the same, or he couldn't belong there.

Rediscovering the river, if it was the same, he fell asleep beside it. Often he appeared to journey in dreams. In sleep he became a stone, sprinkled upon the sodium steppes, dilating in time.

He dreamed again of the river. Ices mingled to a spiked spiral current, desisting to flow yet flowing all the same. Knifing stones and quarries, he traced it with his eyes, on his feet, to the foot of a gigantic jagged sculpture, of natural formation, above a frozen sea, pinions gnashed in shining towers. Jacob bowed beneath it and followed. At the base he touched it, and it was cold, and huge, and solid. Osmosis carried from it, to him, and he became a sculpture, or a castle, or a frost, bracing arctic fountains.

He woke into rumbling; distant, but large and loud, shaking foundations in the very world. A rocky waste succeeded the river, littered with small and larger stones, unanimously gray. Jacob followed these wastes and the noise grew louder. Anticipation froze in him, a larger glacier, and he ran. Wind rushed so furiously he became the sound, and was lifted by it.

An edge formed, and fathoms, and thunder, and he ran through a deep-scarred field, through the rim of giants rising—and stood at the edge of a plateau jutting past the edge of the world, onto an endless torrential waterfall, where distance had no boundaries, and oceans fell into ransacked eternity, bypassing galaxies and cosmic formation… an emptiness entirely without sound, shape or feeling.

::::::::::::::::::

In another version of the tale, when Jacob wakes, he still hears rumbling, but instead of water he grows closer to the base of an immense wall.

Thunder crashed above her; rock melted between arches in the gate. Late light approached but would not be let inside, whereat it began to crawl. Inside existence was made pitiful, and even gods crawled, hyperbolic in infinite pretensions: a conduit for monsters.

Laura became a part of that conduit, and something cold ran down her back, sign of touch or glance or presence. She held one hand against the wall (rough liquid fermenting, sharp as melting iron), strident footsteps affirming *yes she was here* and the flowers had yet to fall. An obstacle knocked her down, and many times she ran into intestinal spikes; but she felt around them if she could walk, and if not, she ducked, or climbed.

The walls reverberated, their particles unstable, weakly groaning. Could this be the cave she remembered, the same destination? She'd come into Jacob's place, his treacherous outcrop, but without him... its blood flowed too deep for her... cool milky chemical blood, carving enactment: a torrent.

This darkness reminded her of a dream she'd had—or a dream within a dream, within a dream. She didn't know whether before or after coming here with Jacob, but she remembered this moment from it. Or maybe this was the dream she remembered, and again she'd passed through time; or she'd always been here.

Detached from senses, she regained awareness of her own body. Despite darkness blood flowed in it, firm and warm, her self within it maybe, defining her in visual space, centering experience. She was here and really here, like nothing. Wherever this took her she would still be there. Or so she hoped.

Already she'd walked much longer than before. The floor sloped to become impossibly steep, and the air thinned, as though it weren't meant to be inhaled, or wasn't air at all. The cave would shrink until it crushed her, so she could be strong stone with a girl on it, spread hyper-long onto trim hallways.

Broadening echoes counteracted her fear, growing so dim it was futile to follow the wall. She must have entered a cavern or large room. Extending her hands to ward off obstacles, she followed them instead, feeling she staggered across a platform in the sky, bathed in darkness and winds.

The sound of dripping water. She went to it, touching a beam the liquid traveled. In a shallow basin, the droplets collected. Her hand grazed it. For a moment (so quick it might never have happened, or might have happened forever) the surface possessed the smoothness of glass, until the glass broke to liquid coolness. She lifted handfuls and drank. Heavy echoes, a cloudscape.

She blinked, and minutiae lights submerged the corridor. Her reflection appeared in the water: soft blue on stunning white, shadowed faintly against the bottom. The spear above the pool had been rock, but turned vitreous in the light, and her image split within it, glittering sporadically. Drops fell from the stalagmite, rippling an ocean.

Submerged in pure whiteness: a giant crystal. Rows of shell-like objects opened in the wall—they weren't really objects, but instead an aspect of transition that went many directions. Perception spun within cerulean corridors, multiplying reflections in an octagon. Clear columns lifted the foundations, resisting the whirlwind. Her image spun, captured in the shells, until she thought maybe that wasn't just her image, but her too, and she looked back at herself, together; searching everywhere—within, outside the universe coagulated to an amorphous, heterogeneous blob—and that shining didn't come off of existence, it *was* existence, duplicating objects and doing away with them, making them everything.

Taking a step (in one sense, just not a physical one) she slipped into that spiral vortex, gravitating into a diamond, tumbled in multiple directions. The diamond morphed to a hexagram, endlessly in flux; the hexagram projected from a single point, but that point hung everywhere, even outside it. She became a turquoise blob sketched lime-green upon a jiggling surface; seeming to watch herself from above, like an object submerged beneath water. Her wriggling, subliminal self reeked of contained growth. Perception panned backwards. She saw another, and that was her too. But outside herself, from within, she felt *something else*, flowing in her, as she flowed with it, parallel to many other things. It wasn't a threatening awareness—they made no distinction in single objects—but she didn't belong here, couldn't *be* here: the swirls spun all wrong, and they tore at her head. The circle linked its edges into a ring, glowing neon colors, until the ring broke, and patterns coagulated (checkered, descending, rebuffing) harshly. She seeped away like a string pulled from tapestry.

Her hand touched the rock, alike to the stalagmite atop; the pool glittered sharp and clear. Dim light seemed to make a sound but didn't. She didn't understand it in relevance to herself. Returning here, everything was imitation.

She saw a stone basin in the center of the room. Within it burned lethargic flame, illuminating a much larger area than she remembered. The walls bore similar markings, just more of them. Angular statues struck strange poses, arms folded impossibly, grotesque teeth pointed from mouths too large, recognizably human but just barely. Stone tapestries laid decorative spans. Display cases (unknowable) stood beside these, carved of some holy substance, the color of the sun.

Here everything was gold, especially the fire. A painted sun shined above it, angular and violent; an eye stared out from the center, lashes curled gently.

The whole room resembled a map of the valley. It had walls, and riches, and the sun, and the right shape, and it gave her a similar feeling. Yet how could there be two of it? There shouldn't, should there?

Except the room had both a cage and a doorway.

The edge of the bowl felt cold and heavy. Beneath green and gold patterns, she saw the symbol she remembered: diagonal black lines, a third piercing the first. Little heat came from the fire, but she suspected it gave off no heat at all. Yellow fell back to lighter orange, transfigured to white, occasionally red. Certain patterns reminded her of herself, of flowers, and she dove alongside them to a floral nutrient abyss, along a rapidly spinning wheel; embers became seeds, stalks flaring transcendentally upwards.

Phantasmagoria berated her, low yet sharp yet equivocally *there*, much like a sound that had never happened, or happened into infinity. It had been soft, seeming to echo intertwining hallways but to have been magnified down them, distorted past a barrier. Another sound, of footsteps; another and she saw Jacob.

The fire stained him dark orange.

He wore different clothes, or maybe memory failed her and they were really the same, like he'd worn the first time, something vaguely resembling a tunic, and walked slowly, arms pressed in various positions to his body, clasping hands then dropping them to his side, blinking once unless Laura imagined it. He stared to the sun, showing nothing in wide dark eyes. Twin statues framed him. He slouched, features smoothly chiseled, as though made of hard water, or painted upon polished stone.

"Where did you come from?" she asked.

Jacob ignored her. He stood a short distance from the painted door, but at that angle, the way he approached, he couldn't have come from there.

He took another step.

She repeated herself, and he did the same.

At the basin, he removed something from one palm, sprinkling it. The flames turned soft green as ash burned away. His first handful disappeared, and he took another. Phantasmagoria masked him. Green fire and rushing wind.

"Where were you?"

She looked at the wall, at Jacob, at the door: looked between them.

He threw more incense, and a rich smell rose, concentrated essence. The flame muffled her voice, becoming louder as she spoke. And taller. At a last, heavy sprinkling, it remained dark green. Wiry smoke curled to dismemberment, and a secondary smoke came from this, invisible but seeming to rise. Emerald ornamentations shone; others wavered purple and burgundy.

"It's a diagram—" Jacob said, and pointed upwards. Instead of an eye she saw the dualistic symbol, an inky impossible black, droplets falling—"of the universe," and traced the pattern with his finger: two sharp arks, and another cutting through. "When the sun looks out through one it sees us," he said, "and we live, and we are; but when it looks out the other, the one that doesn't look the same anymore, what does it see then?"

His slash seemed to carry, and rupture and divide.

Jacob circled the urn, and took her hand softly. His was cold. She wanted to resist, but she listened to Jacob now. He led her towards the doorway, past the cage, and out of herself. The cage was unlocked, but was there something in it? Where had that thing gone? Her head felt lighter than smoke from the fire, and her body drifted without her. If you knew how, Jacob said, it was possible to make the door open.

Gidian wandered until noon. The sun spread its titanic edges—and yes it really got bigger, and maybe warmer too. He removed secondary articles of clothing. It wasn't a painful day, but there was a rough edge on the heat, and the grasslands had begun to resemble a pit of daggers.

He sat outside the ivied temple, its great edge rising three, four times the height of a man, gigantic gates a-taunting, hot dust below him, silent ferns in a phalanx behind. The surface had been polished by eons to relative comfort. There were others there, but he couldn't tell if they had a reason to be, and he hoped they didn't, because neither did he. Together, not speaking, they pondering the towering structure.

Stone lasts longer than wood, even if that lasts very long indeed.

One came towards him. He wasn't old enough to be a man, but not young enough to be a boy. After preliminary greetings, he asked if Gidian remembered him.

Gidian said he didn't.

"We used to play together when we were young," the man explained.

Gidian shook his head, thinking past a movement, behind a surface, he wasn't sure what—the imprints of so many past-selves, minds and habits made nothing. In their haze he seemed to dance at a very young age, cordially exchanging on a hill in the primary valley, but he didn't remember that well either.

"What's it like in there?" the man asked.

Gidian knew he wasn't supposed to talk about it (another unspoken consensus), but he'd never been one to follow rules.

"It's very young," he said, "and beautiful, and quiet," and wind breaks atop obstacles, spears of rock bashing the ground, the world washed in perfect heartbeats, "and when you go there it makes you feel perfect, like you never want to leave. But you always do, and I already have."

Soon after, he excused himself.

The market was empty today, meaning there *was* no market, and he passed through it, discovering places in trees he remembered, of previous combinations. He hadn't kissed a girl in many, many days, despite countless nights sleeping with one. For fear of monsters, he avoided clustered flowers.

Near the wastelands, he found a large hole. He thought to jump down it, but noticed that if he did he might never come up. The sides spread wider than his arms, without handhold, and the bottom went deeper than he was tall, where he saw dry smooth earth, clay-brown, with cracks and small stones in it, and something else too, that he couldn't see. Grass grew up to its very edges, so if he hadn't been observant he might have fallen anyway.

Gidian had grown accustomed to the immobile earth, and didn't like knowing it could be reshaped. Someone could dig down, and down, and down. He didn't know what they'd find, or where they'd come out, or if somewhere below there really was another wall, but above it, foundation for his whole world of petty flowers, was just a layer of pliable earthen dirt, and that scared him.

Probably he should warn the villagers so they knew to be careful, but he couldn't help feeling that if he kept quiet about it maybe it would just go away, as though it were part of him, like a thought, a feeling, that he could so simply ignore, even if those don't go away either. Yet above all, he feared that he might find another.

Something wriggled within his stomach, slithering strangely. Noon had passed but the day remained new. Soon, three children would reemerge from paradise, knowing they'd soon return. He hated himself for thinking like that but he couldn't help it.

He passed by a tree, and found his name carved in it, then an old fence that didn't belong to anyone anymore, jagged and splintered, inconsistent beside the long-curving path. Dashing around a patch of flowers, he went beneath an arch of greenery (a slim wreath, or ring), and in the clearing beyond, near shallow stones, he found Laura.

Her skin, usually tan, had gone pale white; if Gidian had known, he might have compared the tone to Jacob. Her chin jutted the ground, and she hugged herself with both arms. He saw a small black lamp, its handle inches beyond her fingers.

Her eyes opened slowly, but she looked at him, and she was still there, just barely. Lateness dappled her shoulder. With his help—she was very light—she stood; bent to pick up the lamp. She looked around for a moment and asked where they were. Gidian had been here a few days before. He recognized the many entrances, and the equal number of exits, but he had no idea.

He offered to take her home, unsure if she'd be able to make it on her own, and as they walked, her weight draped over his shoulder, he remembered wanting to find her earlier (during the day he'd forgotten exactly what he was looking for) and felt there was something he desperately wanted to ask her; but questions, like secrets, had fallen already into hidden memory. They spoke of many things, but as is the way with conversation, said very little.

At her house—it looked like most any in the village (from outside), but drew attention because of the garden—he let her go. She thanked him more gratefully than he'd expected, considering their past identities. He noticed her empty hands.

"Did you forget something?"

"What?"

"In the clearing you had something with you. I saw you pick it up."

"No," she said, "If I did, I don't remember."

She left, but there was something missing. He returned to the clearing, and though her body had left an imprint in the sand, that was all he found.

Puzzled, pondering the pathways in this place, its overlaps, intersections, he settled (unsatisfied) to play music.

He failed—maybe because the time wasn't right, but more likely the deeper problem was him. He wasn't fit, or capable, and he didn't deserve beauty in the remnants of apocalypse. If someone had listened they might have enjoyed it, but what they heard would be *just* music. After just days, he'd forgotten every old song.

In this life there were things he could never atone for, even without knowing what they were; lateral presence vacating this ancient intersection, more and more as though he only had one foot in the solid universe; could never mesh with it. As night approached—quickly, and with inexplicable speed—he pondered remaining awake, to see the tyrant, the abominable sun, but feared that if he saw it rise, saw it set, it might take it with him into reality's ideographic negative, washed noxious green and florescent purple, fully commensurating that separation, making him nothing.

He fell asleep beneath barrage, another break in linear sequence, as dusk flung arrows and wavelengths—or he must have—dreaming of this same clearing at the same time of day, amidst pouring, but it was younger, and there were people there. The lump of stones had become an altar once more, where many prayed. Others conversed in groups, or formed a short line. In Gidian's time, there had never been worship like this. In Gidian's time, there was no such thing as worship.

He joined the nearest group. He didn't expect to be noticed; when he was (by a young girl approximately his age: she had almost boy-short brown hair, and wore a thin shirt that exposed her slim arms) he could barely think past the frightening lucidity of the dream.

Her image wavered, and perception spun throughout the clearing. He heard every conversation, seeing everyone.

"Oh," he said. "Hello."

"I've never seen you before," she said. "Hello."

"What's your name?"

She told him

Gidian thought she would ask his own, but it never crossed her mind.

"Where did you come from?"

"The future, or maybe the past. I think I'm dreaming, but I'm not sure. Sometimes it's hard to tell, especially for me. Maybe I'm looking for something. Probably."

She pointed. "Is this it?"

"It is."

By her ankle, lying inverted where she'd left it, he saw Laura's lamp. It hung awkwardly by the handle, refusing to straighten. He repeated, "Yeah, this is it."

"It doesn't belong here."

"Neither do I."

"Lay down with me. I'll take you home."

They did. She put herself on top of him and her hands on his wrists, gently, as though she were made of water, or wind, and when she kissed him it seemed he fell into those waves, into a portal she opened. As he fell, he lost his grip on the lantern. Though he reached out, it had been lost in the whirlwind, and he sank beneath her, or floated.

He awoke at night's last vanishings. He didn't see the flash of the sun itself, but instead the light it cast, mixing so many colors as to have no color; by the time he looked to the sky, it had returned to a single point, winking eventually open.

He felt for the lamp. It was still gone, any markings obscured by his grasping hands. But as pockmarks filled with shadows, across the clearing, he could have sworn he saw footprints; and—though it might just have been his siftings in sleep—perhaps, the indent of another body beside his own.

For three days, Jacob stayed at the edge of the world. Thought turned to perpetual roaring. The emptiness gave him only itself, as though he had given something already, that could never be returned or replaced—his heart, his soul, or his self—stained glass in that worthless piece of crystal. He might never leave: become a rock perched upon the magnesium cliffs, eroded by wind.

As the landscape fell back, so too did that roar.

He came to a desert near the rim, one he had not crossed before, or not noticed crossing… the body of a God dead trillions upon trillions of days, whom had left only his frozen skin, his arctic decay. The ground flaked, becoming plates and tiles; minerals laced the rock, much like those along the edge (crustal greenery and clawed hands)—or he thought them minerals, as opposed to plain stones, for reasons he was unable to explain.

Here, passage was slower than the plains, having lost that precious object. His reflection, dappled on glass. Irony seemed a joke but he wasn't laughing; he hated these dark purple wastes, their crevices across evil rock; that monstrosity obscured by cloud, battered by lightning. In sleep, he returned there—but this time he jumped, hung suspended after space ceased to matter, soul carried by messengers to the far corner of nothing (nothing in rapturous arcs, nothing in his unnatural shell); his flesh unwound like a tapestry of stars, as threads took the place of his veins….

He woke into familiar monotony, thirsting for the first time in his life, hungered for the longest time imaginable. So familiar was the awakening that he might never have been to the edge at all. Such that he might continue on, to verify memory—but either he would return to that azure waste, or he would go nowhere at all, and neither appealed to him.

So he turned towards home.

In returning, he might follow the river, knowing (hoping) on where it might lead him—if this was the same river, and if he'd come from anywhere at all; or he could turn, and set out for another valley entirely. There are many directions he might have taken, infinite permutations upon those given above, and many things he might have found. Some he might have found before, but have gone without mention for the sake of coherence. Yet it may be that Jacob never went any of these places. If so, most certainly not in this order.

:::::::::::::::::

He spent days in sparse vegetation, the omnipresent grasses: leafy abscess, worn frame, threaded into frequent stones. His joints swelled and hardened—a mutant toughness, aching liquid inside—and his skin was like poorly made paper. The bones bent beneath it.

On the second day (or the first, or the third) the land broke into long, scarred patches. Nothing grew upon them, and their soil did not clump; it was more dust than soil.

Further out, he saw waves.

He explored one approximately the size of the valley, or a bit larger. Within, the earth had grown so fine it resembled a sea. Steps took him first to his ankle, then his knees, and finally further, until he fell—past himself into the surprisingly warm earth, that crawled powdery in his eyes, that flowed grainy in the mouth, past the feeble membrane, past life, into a place where everything sank, where sinking was eternity.

Perniciously afloat, limpidly drifting, he recalled his vision upon escaping the valley—if it had really been a dream—and returned to it, taking a body with him this time. He soared, blazing in darkness; within the pressurized earth, he might fall in many directions, without filtered light, choked and hungered. But remembering another dream, he imagined himself underwater, suspended now as he was approached by the mouth of a gigantic beast, or lumbering vessel. It was coming, he thought. It would come.

The water shook, and he began to rise—but continued to struggle, so perhaps he rose of his own power, while imagining the rumble. His fingers arched and seemed to grasp stars: he caught them, surfaced in a soft pool, sickly smooth. He swam upwards (the dirt was too thin to grab) unto walls; submerged to his sandy, sandy shoulders. He scaled a waterfall (it spat powder) and became a pile beside it.

Sleep tumbled him, and in the distance—a desert—he saw an animal risen in plumes become mist as it fell.

It roared, and shook, and the waves split to make its way.

He awoke in the calm, the shallows. His footprints were gone; had taken destination with them. He sensed wind but doubted it would have erased his trail so quickly, unless he'd slept a day and *night; so without him knowing, the creature must have taken him to a different area of the field entirely—or impossible currents had dragged him.*

With little practice, he learned to widely disperse his weight, or crawl. It took much longer to leave than enter, but he experienced no further difficulty.

The border was without landmark, and he had forgotten any direction. Had he departed, he might rediscover the river, or another river entirely, but it was unlikely. Mountains owned the distance: thin, crooked cones, strung and clustered. They had the power to shape the land around them, and were soon to disappear. Sometimes, because they always looked the same, he suspected there was only one range of mountains, that moved.

He slept next to a stone, but did not wake next to one.

For days he found nothing else, but learned to follow. Perhaps, if he'd left the river, without discovering another, he might regret making the decision. The air grew warmer so that he might walk naked to feed—yet he starved still.

For days he slept only beside landmarks, favoring the stone cones. One in three mornings, a tree or bush might remain, but never the cone. As an object increased in significance (to him?) so then did its rate of movement (he looked to the mountains, the horizon).... But perhaps the ratios only differed, and one day, if he slept by a cone (perhaps one in six, or nine, even ten, eleven—after this the number exceeded his ability to count, but that didn't keep in from being*) it might* not *move. Yet this theory grew problematic also, as if he discarded the horizon as an object, what did he make of the ground or the sky—and more important, why had he never lost the river?*

Before sleep, he thought again of changing his course; even, if possible, returning to the river. He woke, and yet another cone had disappeared: the fourth. Seeing this, and sliding, he refused to think that maybe it wasn't that landscape that moved, but he—but did it?

On the sixth day he woke to a sky only lit on far distant sides, and especially dark. Boulders rolled within it, and though it hung beyond vision, shaded by cloud, he sensed a coiled beast that slid in weightless stony scales, a king of thunder and light, despite the presence of neither. Jacob suspected that no matter how long he remained, that darkness would be there longer, hunting ground of that serpentine monster.

Most noticeable, yes, was the feel of not belonging, of having fallen somewhere lower, or different, past a gap in the patterns (his pass between movement), and from it he drew his conclusions, believing in thunder.

Just beyond him (if he trusted memory, it was in the same location as the cone the previous night) Jacob saw an old, old building, its foundations of stone, its walls and windows of stone, steps and stairways decrepit amidst a playground of shadows. The earth around it differed from memory, more heavily scarred. Over the entrance—if there had ever been a door, it was gone now—he saw the scratch-faded remnants of some crest: sick pinkish red, vaguely resembling an eye but with a hook in place of the pupil.

The floor was dirt, devoid of footprints, but Jacob added his own. Light slanted precariously—it came from two windows, on opposite sides of the dwelling—crossing like the ends of the serpent. There was no roof, but the floor of the second level covered almost half of the first. In the corner, dirt rose, leading to a stairway. Beside those, a flat outcrop might conceivably have been a table, or bed, but he doubted both. The bricks were like hardened mud, and he feared they might melt. He touched them, and his finger returned filmed in a chalky substance.

He feared climbing the stairs, but did so without trouble.

Broad windows showed him panorama and shattered horizon, bleeding white, the destroyer of this secondary, underlying world. Between the windows: a row of benches, also rectangular, and between these a square altar. In the past lifetimes, the dust within might have conceivably been ashes.

Proceeding exploration, the building seemed a shrine of some sort. The furnishing was too sparse to warrant a constant residence, as was the location—at least in present times, despite being along the river—yet perhaps this was only from a different, more restrained era, one that still endeavored to worship.

But he had trouble believing in the place. It belonged here even less than he—seemed to have been created for him, even created by him; that lifestyle, whether clerical or domestic, could only belong to his father. If this place were the correct age, with stones like these, it would be dust. Dust and memory.

He left, and walked long in alien lands, into the white-burning horizon. But when he awoke, in a place he seemed to remember, it was at the base of an immense mountain.

Laura returned home as in a dream, and spoke within a dream to a stranger. She watched him leave through the window, hoping he might pause to look at her garden. Through that, he might have made her beautiful. But he never even turned.

A voice spoke from behind her.

"Oh," she said. "Michelle. Hi."

"You look tired."

"I am."

"And you look sad too."

"A little." Laura paused, and held her hands together. She shut her eyes. "I'd rather not talk about it."

"How many days has it been now?"

"I couldn't count if I tried."

She paused, turned, and wanted very badly to send her head hurtling past the wall, into a dark place, where there was no thinking, and all she had to do was watch, or wonder, as so many things unraveled about her.

She thought she might turn into the kitchen, but no, she went toward the couch, and her sister followed.

Like most homes without artists, Laura's was primarily bare, even if it had a second floor. Before the windows, dust sprinkled aloft, billowing past the curtains.

"Have you noticed how loud the floor is?" Laura took a step; she noticed.

"Sometimes."

"It's like that upstairs too. But not at other peoples' houses, except Jacob's."

"Maybe ours has another room," Michelle said. "A secret one."

They sat together. Michelle held both arms around her knees, shielded by a blanket. A rug—also very rare for being colored, unlike the blanket—covered the floor beneath Laura's feet. It had been sewn out of some fiber or another, from the belly of a special plant.

"We sure do have lots of nice things," she said.

"I guess."

Laura lifted her knees to her chest. If someone had been watching, for the first time in a long time, maybe ever, she and Michelle looked like sisters. "Sometimes I don't trust them. Our parents, I mean. Have you ever wondered where they go?"

"Not really."

"Sometimes I forget how old I am. You haven't always been here."

"Do you know where they go?"

"If I did," Laura said, "I don't think I could tell you." But sometimes, more than anything about her parents, her sister, her family, she wondered if she was even herself; and if not, at where the rest of her had gone.

Michelle coughed, blinking her eyes.

"Are you crying?"

"If I was," Michelle said, "I wouldn't tell you either."

"Why?"

"The things you say sometimes."

"I didn't know you cared."

"Normally I don't. Most of the time."

"Here." Laura gestured to the blanket. "Wipe your eyes."

"Sometimes it's like we aren't people at all."

"Sometimes we aren't."

"We're like blankets, just we don't keep people warm."

"Wipe your eyes, or you'll stain your clothes"

"It's not you." Michelle's voice quivered. "When I come here in the evening it makes me sad. It's too quiet."

"I know. Now wipe your eyes."

"You're right. Sometimes it's like we aren't even sisters."

"Even if we weren't, I would love you like one."

"That's not true."

"Maybe not, but I meant it when I said it, and I still do."

"When I come here in the evening," Michelle repeated, "it makes me sad."

::::::::::::::::::

That night Laura boiled something with potatoes and carrots in it, accompanying the two with another fried vegetable—a sort of spicy cabbage. Both dishes she dashed with herbs, none of which she'd grown herself, because she only grew flowers. No one noticed that though her flowers looked pretty they didn't have a use. Like her they didn't have a use.

Michelle ate quietly. She refused to look anywhere but her plate. The table had two empty sides for her parents: as always, empty.

"What would you think," Laura said, "if they never came back?"

"Nothing."

"I could take care of you. Sometimes I do that already, like now."

"You wouldn't want to. And I wouldn't want you to, either."

"Don't say that." Laura took a spoonful of soup. "You shouldn't."

"It's true."

"Only because you say it is."

"If it were up to you," Michelle said, "everything would be a lie."

Laura wasn't hungry anymore. She never ate large amounts, and neither did Michelle. They were like flowers, she thought, who drank only water, feasting upon sunlight. Except she didn't get that anymore either.

"What happened to you?"

"When I sit at home in the evening," Michelle repeated, "it makes me sad."

"If you say so."

"Did you hear that Gidian's parents were going to have another child?"

"How?"

"I'm not sure. I bet they're disappointed in him, because he's himself."

"It's not true. They won't."

"Why?"

"I'm not sure if it can be done."

"It can, probably, or else how did we get here?"

::::::::::::::::::

Where are you? Laura asked. It's like you've gone somewhere.

I'm here right now, aren't I?

I'm not sure who you are, or who you were, either.

That's okay. Sometimes I'm not sure myself.

:::::::::::::::::::

She came awake, and met with an enemy, but what had she forgotten? Two spread hands: she looked at them. What did they do, and did they have the capability to hold?

She slept, and might have found the answer in a dream. But instead found only her front room. Darkness pressed about the windows. She mulled upon loose floorboards. In lifting one (she could do that, because they weren't stuck down, didn't belong, like sticks for her to step between) what might she find below?

One she removed—it clicked—and gave to the floor without impact. It formed the beginnings of a pile. Below, blackness filled a narrow window. Closer, she removed another board, and another, until the floor had a gigantic hole in it, bigger than her or anything previous.

In the kitchen, she noticed a stairway. Its steps led to a doorway. Either she'd forgotten, or never seen it before, but knew irrefutably that it would take her into a secret place, where she'd never been. Maybe babies came from there: the place beneath floorboards.

To reach the stairs, she would have to jump over the hole, and that scared her. She replaced a board, or tried, but it fell—when she turned for another, they were all gone.

Her steps spread ripples in the quaking foundation. She clung to the wall, but that rippled too.

She staggered.

And jumped: but that jump was a continuation of her previous motion, without height, strength, or distance. There she hung—limp, frame suspended upon wires—knowing that soon she would fall; even if she landed (which she wouldn't) the roots would shoot upwards, and collapse, and come with her into that great oily nothingness.

She fell into herself; waking, struggled against blankets; struggling, tumbled from the mattress to the floor. Her skull ricocheted and hurt. She clung to woven softness, convinced somehow that she still fell: and did.

Light tore the window, a colorless mesh, breaching fundament. It was the glassy sheet past which she slid, but when it slipped, where did it leave *her*?

She climbed the stairs slowly, carrying a pillow and dragging her head. The room from her dream was still dark. Her steps did not shake the doorway—she attempted many times to verify this, pausing at the aperture between kitchen, living room, and doorway.

Space shifted in places hidden.

"Michelle, are you here?"

A silent motion repeated—she faced it, and something rose from Michelle's sofa, whirling softly; the creature vaguely resembled the younger girl, but it had dark holes in place of its eyes (red slivers within them) and transparent skin.

"No," it said. "She hasn't been here for a long, long time."

Laura shook. "Who are you?"

"Remember." She didn't. "Many times I've known you before."

Never.

"When you were a little girl," it said, "I took you on walks through the tyrant valley, and we swam together in long rivers. I made skeleton marks on you, and licked the mercurial blood that came from them. One day at a time, so you didn't notice, I took a bite off your soul, until gradually there was nothing left."

The wraith hovered. Both arms hung untethered to its body; an open mouth conquered half the face. The torso leaked smoke, gyrating. A tattered dress clung upon crisped wrinkles.

"Is she asleep?" Laura asked. "Michelle, I mean."

"No."

"Did she ever come home last night?" Laura picked up the nearest object—a decorative platter—and brandished it, suddenly chill, feeling she stood against wind. That laughter belonged to something else. Yes, she considered, it looked startlingly like Michelle, but it had fangs, and vortex, and inhumanity. "Where is she now?"

"Not here."

"Answer me."

"You don't have the power."

Answer me.

"If you look hard enough," it pointed at her—pointed *through* her—to a corner, the far kitchen wall, that she remembered from her dream, "you might find a stairway."

"What do you want?"

"I require tribute, but you don't have anything left to give."

"I could give you flowers," Laura said, "but you aren't worthy to take them."

And then:

"You don't look anything like my sister."

"I don't pretend to."

"You don't belong here, and you shouldn't say things like that."

It grinned—sickly—and she seemed to see right past it: azure tinged black and ice crystals sliding slowly apart, beaded with droplets. One fell, as did she, and something broke in the distance, or below her. Her head ached; peristalsis vacated thought, impeding the gates between her and existence, their cool river flowering past solids… that river froze, and she became a stalagmite, imprisoned within dark crystal, careening in harsh clouds. She broke the surface of an ocean, laced with acid, or needles: soul hurtled against the sodium reefs, their crags framed in negative shades, strong against somnolent storms. Obscured by salt, cut into billionths, she swam this torrent, to find it populated by demons, void of shelter and warmth; wishing only that she might rise—or descend—from this seething sky, its perpetual rain, its spires flooding in nothing, its sun a hole to pour energy; but when she lifted her hands (her nothing) they were gone, like everything: a gyration amidst stars, which cannot move, and will never do so.

:::::::::::::::::::

She woke beneath Michelle's blanket. Light invaded the windows. Encountering it, she blinked, and sought to recede fully into her core and warmth. She failed; failed again; stood, the blanket hanging from her, and went to the kitchen. Its corners belonged to dust and other infinitesimal things.

She changed clothes and left to bathe; returned carrying a piece of fruit whose name she didn't know. Her teeth pierced flavored chambers, delightfully cool, crisp, and sweet. The valley contained more varieties of fruit than it did people, just as it held more flowers by far, but only a few trees. It had enough room to fit many, many people, but there were barely half of a hundred, at most.

Michelle must have gone last night, after Laura had fallen asleep. Laura (almost) missed her. Thinking back to their conversation, she wondered, if their parents never came back, *could* she take care of Michelle…? (and was there any love?) She'd meant it at the time but she couldn't mean it now, certain, now irrevocably so, that in truth they had left long ago, and she would never see them again, even from bushes.

Today would be a good day, she decided. Until yesterday, upon telling yet another lie, she really had kept track of the day, and thought every morning of where she might be, and where she'd been, and who would be there right now: a littler, more important version of herself, upholding history to make herself feel beautiful, as in its absence she could never feel again.

Outside, sun scorched the fields, blazing white in the gardens. The light was too strong, impossibly bright; she put a hand before her eyes and a wavelength bent, curled into created space. She wanted to tend her garden, but she couldn't. The light was less like heat than an arrow, something more frightening, like gravity.

Last night, before sleep, there had been something important, some memory, thought or reflection. It flickered; she blinked. But now, as then, she lost it. It wasn't something she could pick up, set down, or pretend to hold. In its absence she became a statue, unwilling to think something else: that it had been taken from her. She couldn't believe that. Not now. Maybe never.

Gidian decorated piled stones. Hearing footsteps, he lifted his hat towards them. The sun reflected off it, not reaching him past the brim but scouring the world around, suspended in brilliance, sage and altar.

"What are you doing here?" Laura asked.

"I came back after walking you home," he said. "It was getting dark, so I slept here too. When I woke up, I left to get breakfast. I stayed at home for a while, then I came back, because I like it here."

"It seems like I find you everywhere."

"I hadn't noticed."

"You wouldn't. Normally I leave." She paused. "Sometimes I don't like you very much. I'm not sure if you know."

"I do," Gidian said. "You make it obvious."

"Not on purpose."

Gidian stopped. He was still unaccustomed to basic conversation. That meant giving his full attention to another person, or giving it at all. Others made it look much less difficult than it was.

He asked what she'd come back for.

"To see if I'd forgotten anything."

And him?

"I'm not sure," he said—it didn't feel like a lie. At the time he'd been looking for something, and he told her so, but it couldn't be so simple. Nothing else was. "Then it seemed like a good place to sleep—but I have another reason, and I don't remember what it was. I might be able to tell you later. Right now, it's somewhere else. Not here.

"Over that hill," he pointed, "I watched the sun rise. Today it got bigger than ever before, or closer. I'm sure you noticed. And this morning, it seemed like a great place to sit. It's very quiet here."

She said: "I thought it was just me."

"I'm not sure if the sun moves," he said, "but that would explain the extra heat. But if it had gotten larger, the same would be true."

"Maybe we could ask Jacob's father," Laura said, "but I don't like the idea. He wouldn't tell us anything. It wouldn't be safe, either."

"Or it might have gotten stronger," he continued, "the light itself, I mean. That would make it bigger, and hotter. But it wouldn't have to move, or change size."

"It might not do any of those things, even if it was true."

"We'd have to assume it would," Gidian said, "because it's already happened. If not, it isn't even an option."

Laura shrugged. "It might just be us—the people, I mean. Everything else is the same, but because we're different, we're seeing it different, like it is."

"I doubt it."

"Why?"

"Through it all, every day, we've been here. But sometimes, the sun goes invisible, and things might happen to it. It if was us, we would know, but with the sun, we wouldn't." He stood, lifting an object from his pelvis. "It doesn't go both directions."

Laura blinked. "I thought you broke that."

"No, I've had it for days now. It's different, or not the same. Maybe I've always had it."

"Can you still play?

"I've forgotten all my old songs." He held it into the light, mourning them. "That other me, the one who played better, when I lost my instrument, he went with it."

"It looks similar. Maybe a little smaller."

"But it isn't." He turned, as though to leave. Maybe he intended to, but he didn't know. "It looks the same but it just isn't."

"Where are you going?"

"I'm not sure."

A tower spired above them—to Gidian it was shaped like the rough trunk of a tree, peaking into branches; they curved into claws, grasping the sky—eclipsing tall trees, all extremity. He looked closer, and everything melted. He stared, wondering if Laura had seen (she said nothing); at how much he'd imagined.

She put a hand on his arm—to stop him, he realized. It didn't feel right for her to touch him, but it didn't feel bad either. "Won't you stay?"

"You could come with me," he offered.

"No." She stepped back, clasping both hands. "I don't think I can.

"Are you sure?" She refused his hand. She took another step.

"Sometimes I'm not sure about anything."

He nodded. "Sometimes, neither am I."

:::::::::::::::

Gidian cast his image upon the water. The reflection, even disregarding current, hardly resembled him. It was older and harsher, chiseled like that of a warrior. His own, secret, personal self still had long hair, fair skin, and none of the gashes he saw. For a moment, he hoped the surface lied, or that he could cast away his roughness like yet another self, but it wasn't so easy.

His lifted the instrument. He'd like to say *his* instrument, but that couldn't be true anymore. Playing, he conversed with strangers. The strength, the purpose of memory had gone. Even on simple melodies he fumbled. It was too heavy to hold, and he remembered her comment: it wasn't the other that had changed, but he. No, in this life he could never accept that.

Belatedly, he recalled something he'd wanted to ask, concerning Michelle. He'd forgotten the question, but could only hope some opportunity reminded him. Discovering her the morning before last—it couldn't have been this day, having awoken in the clearing—he'd overlooked it, but even then he'd wanted to ask, or take her with him.

She might be home. He didn't choose to go there, but went regardless. Despite the early light, he passed no one. The instrument came with him, but he didn't deserve to carry it, he didn't have the strength. He visited his own home first, abandoning such weight. Yet in a sense, it came with him still.

He paused beside the garden to marvel at its winding body, woven of living patterns, blush and color; voluptuous as the body of a woman, a cumulative bloom, stems becoming arms, legs and torso, petals becoming eyes. It couldn't be beautiful like a real woman, but it brimmed with the wakened vibrance of living gardens, a new creature entirely.

The door was tall and wide, of strong pale wood. Laura's had always been a nice house, almost as nice as his, pitifully rivaled by the neighbors—suddenly with a poignant hope that they didn't take it as such, yet knowing they surely did—and nowhere in the world could one find the equivalent of this garden.

He knocked twice. Laura opened the door. Her eyes widened, her mouth opened, but he read nothing in them. Had she always been so opaque? He didn't think so, but perhaps, again, the change took place not in her but him.

The entrance swung open. She wore different clothes.

"Is Michelle here?" he asked.

"You came here to talk to her?" Laura blinked, shaking her head. "Really?"

"I think I might love her." He looked at the ground; the floor; at anything. "I'm not sure, but I think I might."

"You don't. Not really."

"Probably not. I don't know. I doubt it."

"Anyway," Laura said, "she's not here. I haven't seen her since yesterday. Even before that. I never pay much attention to her."

"She's very attractive."

"Lots of people think so. Or so I've heard."

"There was something else. I wanted to ask her a question, about one of you. I don't remember what. Maybe I've confused it with something else. With something."

And then: "Are you alright?"

"After I came home," she stepped outside, "I tried to take care of my flowers," and moved towards them, "but they didn't make me happy anymore."

"I'm sorry." He stood aside to let her pass, but she never went anywhere. "I guess I know the feeling."

"Have you ever thought that we don't belong here?" She gestured apparently at random, but he understood, even as he pretended those thoughts away. "I wanted to say we don't belong here *now*, as though there were a time when we did, but I really mean ever. Like never."

She ceased to speak. He looked at her house, past the doorway; then at the garden, the sky; and finally back to her, as if to find a connection, invisible. "Have you been crying?"

"I don't think so." She wiped an eye: large, and tinged with long lashes. "But maybe."

"Do you remember why?"

"If I did, I don't think I would tell you."

"You wouldn't have to." He shivered without understanding why, and clasped her hand tightly. "You don't owe me anything."

She stared. She stood.

She said, "Michelle never came back last night."

"You told me that already. Are you sure?"

She trailed off, looking down, and within her (bypassing connection) he dared the shards of a loose, expanded universe, trailing in icy time, sheared by dust and particles. In that place, he wondered if he could love her—by that, what he meant was save her—but the answer to both questions was no, even with the possibility that he might fall, that they were falling together.

She said, "The night Jacob left. Do you remember where we went?"

"That was a long, long time ago. I was barely even there."

"I think he took part of us with him. He lost them somewhere, and never brought them back." She lifted both hands to her collar, as if to clasp them, but didn't. "And wherever we put the rest, the parts he didn't take, I don't know where to find them. They're somewhere here but I don't know where to find them."

"Don't worry. We will."

"You're a liar." She pushed against his chest. "Everything you say is a lie."

::::::::::::::::::

We need to protect this place. There's a monster, and it eats flowers.

::::::::::::::::::

Gidian imagined much, with barely half of himself in the physical. Like never before, he could see, but it didn't matter anymore. The sky split double, or triple, or nothing. Divided light birthed dual colors. The sun shone in two, and towards it rose a tall, dark pillar.

Pondering much, he seemed to sleep; woke into that same unilateral time. The sun rose, but did not set: distended. Too melancholic to sing, he ate two pieces of fruit.

Satiated, if mildly nauseous, he returned to the pathways. There, he encountered another youth, who ran quickly, and sweated. He wore a wide band around his forehead, between short hair and tanned skin. Gidian recognized him as the village courier, supposedly a novelty.

"There's a meeting," came his message, delivered past staccato breath, "at the center of the village, at the altar." According to Gidian's memory, that place was little more than a relic.

"What's going on?"

"There's a messenger," the boy exclaimed "come down from the sun!"

Jacob became a mountain pillar.

Though featureless as anything else in the world, they were featureless in the vertical, displaying the world from high, high above. While not seeing more, he did see further—and stared to ascertain whether, just maybe, he might encounter the end of flat surfaces, or the marks of a garden.

He slept on a crag overlooking the grasslands. Spotting a tree, he marked the direction with pebbles, but found neither in the morning. His own location had changed as well. The sides and pathways differed in addition to the mountains themselves. At no point did he attempt to memorize locations, or his paths between them. They shifted so suddenly that he might turn at any moment into displacement; look forward to see that changed also. All without sound or apparent movement.

These mountains might once have been habitable. He hoped to find a cave, or a dwelling, so he searched primarily in the valleys. Occasional rivers ran through them. He drank, and the water tasted like water, so it might be the river he knew—but in his experience water had always tasted like water, regardless of location, because it was still water.

The stone was the same brown clay as the cones, and the mountains had a similar shape, so that they might have been the same cones magnified to gigantic proportion, and stood in a grand cluster. He chipped off chucks of the substance; crushed, it ran through his fingers like earth. This softness proved hazardous when it crumbled beneath his feet, but he escaped serious injury.

More than the peaks themselves, he feared where they might take him. Even the land had changed color as it fluctuated between degrees of rockiness. If on foot he'd been headed towards the valley, he had certainly turned from it now, and one morning he might wake to find no mountains at all. He hadn't eaten in many days. Grown increasingly thin, he fed only on the sun, and a weak one at that. The mountains gave him water, but he'd found no trace of mosses.

After many days, recognizing fields resembling those he'd encountered before, he left, not enriched by the mountains but given strength by them. The mountains were tough, and strong, and fast, and silent. If he brought something with him, without leaving too much behind, who knew where it would take him?

He passed along the sands, afraid to enter but hoping he might witness the familiar monster: a dune collapsing. Day did the same, taking with it much distance, and Jacob realized these couldn't be the same fields, they were much too large. The soil was too light for earth. More and more, he thought them remnants ground to powder, or even buried. Before, had he fallen, they might have rested together.

The journey fell into familiar patterns, an absence of destination and object. Jacob imagined a current in himself, and rode upon it, flowing endlessly, flowing forever, to no place of calm water.

There was nothing real in this space, or so he thought, but he had been wrong in the past, and was especially so now. The discovery returned him to himself. He halted, wondering what to consider; at where he'd taken himself. Perhaps his soul had ridden past the boundaries of creation, and rode still, without him.

The object, what remnants he saw, seemed a crumbled formation. Rubble littered the base, still splayed where it had fallen. He recognized the stone—it was much like that of the temple at the center of the valley. Only the pedestal remained in decent condition, though its edges had withered also.

It must have been a carving of sorts. Despite the erasure of all detail, vaguely human proportions remained. Or he assumed they were human. Upon observation of the fragments below, its lower half was too thick to have been anything but a dress. Yet the aura, if he called it that, was decidedly masculine, that of withered, wretched strength. He imagined the statue as it might have been, arm extended over its city (surer and surer the fields had been cities), brow arched in proclamation. Perhaps it had held a weapon in one hand, and people knelt below it....

Jacob considered camping here, but wondering if he might find similar objects, perhaps ones more well preserved, he continued along the strands. The sky stretched behind him, parallel to anything below. But he found nothing that day, and lay down by a large rock. Despite pondering the statue incessantly, as he had done since its discovery, he did not dream.

He awoke on a plank of solid stone, as he'd seen within the previous building. Ovular stone encased him: a jagged, brick-like pattern. Juggled illumination invaded the windows, a diagonal slash upon the walls. He dangled his feet off the platform; they touched no floor. Alongside three others, one set into each wall, it was the only noticeable feature.

Breaching the rim of the doorway, he discovered the outskirts of an abandoned city. Gray buildings spangled the garrulous horizon. There he saw more still, astronomically larger, a patterned array. The soil was soft, and of a similar color, but not the dust from the empty field. Where had sleep taken him? He recognized the landscape somewhat, but land everywhere was the same.

The building in which he'd rested—that was its only purpose, as far as he could tell—appeared unremarkable in the midst of its brothers, all twins. It had only one window; next to that, a large, open doorway. Spiked pins covered the roof, each half his own height. In combination, the structures seemed in suspended animation: ferocious, sleeping creatures, their legs curled beneath the foundations, each one cell of a mobile fortress....

Built seemingly at random, the squatting constructions formed a personalized maze, growing progressively narrower as he approached the city. Certain others, taller and thinner, notched oddly near the top, stood interspersed between them, sat upon by thousands. He saw nothing within his capability to explain, merely a thin pillar running into a shallow rounded put, ringed by seats. Men might have congregated to drink and converse, but nothing beyond that.

He passed a boundary, and another design took the place the original. It was of rectangular construction, with flat rooms and shimmering walls. Despite sparse furnishing, he recognized the elements of a dwelling, and even pits for fire. That night he slept in one, exhausted, but he slept poorly, sight scarred by the far, silent city.

At an even greater distance, the structures changed again: larger, with slightly more space between them, some even had a second floor, and even the smallest were larger than any he'd passed so far. Still, their features were entirely carved out of stone. Strange patterns decorated the walls, geometric and absolutely without meaning.

Ahead, the skyline curved upwards. He passed a new layer each day, proportion escalating in stages. Within them, nothing moved—or if so, only the buildings themselves, and not he within them. Come further, he felt he had been in a large hole in rocky, rocky ground.

Finally, nearing the center, Jacob entered the city: a horror of palaces and freakishly curved archways, spires wrestling with heaven. Each had an interior like a dark cave: winding stair and innumerable paths, which if entered he would never escape. All were empty, and despite many carvings, he saw nothing human within them.

The street spread long, wide, narrow, desolate. Beside it continued the horror of those mansions, a wilderness of stone. No wind reached him, but currents, captured whole eons ago, sounded their whistles within corridors. Harsh darkness fell on him, and he strode perpetually in shadow, his sky a sequence of pillars, his world a nightmare. Pretentious apertures, without rail or stairway, rose amidst a geometric array, and the pillars—long, thin, black cylinders—rose exponentially higher than these, infinitely further than the walls. Never did he see the base of them. He imagined they would be quite large, and without entrance.

Despite previous hope, he saw no statues. This place had nothing human about it; must have belonged to a race of monsters, drowned in sickness, with no inner soul, no connection to others. Exploring other buildings, he found nothing, having gone past the point of contemplation. Pressure crushed the thought out of him, and he ran in madness.

He slept in whatever labyrinth he found, clinging weakly his knees, imagining he drew pictures on the old, quiet walls. He'd come too far to turn back, and without the sun he would die of thirst as well as hunger. Occasional light broke holes in the net above, but it was always too far to reach. In the past there had been glorious clarity, a sequence of mirrors and similar magnifying devices, their unnatural textures turning space to a super-clarity like water. Inside it, all things glowed.

In dreams, those he had, part of him had returned to the plains. A great rainbow arched the horizon, its edges fluctuating with solar hues; awake, he moved towards it also, stumbling close-eyed in the invisible city. Soft warmth tingled within him.

He would never escape the city, but his dream took its place, and soon replaced it entirely. Lightness buoyed him forwards, and he wondered if somewhere, in whatever corner, his cold flesh still lay, froth dried at the corner of its mouth, bleached of all color, with absolutely no spark in that clear piece of crystal.

The river flowed beside him, a pathway to that majestic rainbow arch. Golden hues (a radiant span, the breath of fulminating skies) poured upon it. He drank deeply, and walked without sleep, past obstacles to the quiet interior.

Upon returning to the valley, there are three things he might have seen:

First, and least likely, he saw the sun as he had always seen it: a distant hole in the far empty sky, contained and belonging there, its wide rend unblocked by cloud, framed in blue firmament;

Second, he might have seen the sun as an extension of the sky, much like the pillars he'd seen within the city, seeming to emerge from an impossible distance while extending downward like a dagger;

Third, perhaps the sun was a heavy sphere, descending, as though by its great weight, ever closer to the valley below.

Above them scoured the spectator sun, garbling the evening. The ceremonial space took up a large portion of the hill, but not large enough. Laura wanted to stand outside the crowd, but no such place existed. As such, she stood within it, conversing occasionally but mainly listening to the conversations of others, who had very little to say—feeling much like she'd returned to an alien country, where the world shifted.

A small girl approached her. Momentarily Laura thought it was Michelle, because she had the same hair, but she also had different colored eyes, and not half the boldness. Or Laura would have said Michelle was bold, but that was only because they were sisters. Really, they were much the same size. That girl might have been herself, or she might have been anyone else, too.

She asked if Laura knew what was going on.

"Everyone else seems to," she elaborated, "but all I know is that we were supposed to come here. I followed a friend, but they were running too fast to tell me. Now they're gone, but they didn't know either."

Without waiting for an answer, she continued: "You're Laura, aren't you? The girl from the ritual?"

The girl said more, but Laura interrupted her and excused herself, traveling to a place so deep, so dangerous, that maybe no one recognized her, or so she hoped.

Arriving there, she found Gidian.

"Oh," he said. "There you are."

"Were you looking for me?"

"No, but this place is so small, I thought I might find you anyway." He gestured at the edges. "It's obvious why no one comes here anymore. I wouldn't." Adjacent to his shoulder, Laura saw the temple, very large—and then the place of welcome, where they stood, that wasn't.

The crowd pressed them against each other, much of that conversation having taken place not face to face, but torso to torso. Laura didn't like feeling herself against him—though it wasn't his fault, it was just him *plus* her that she didn't like—and one of them, she couldn't tell whom, was enjoying it too much. She turned so they stood shoulder to shoulder. Her elbow pressed into his stomach, and Gidian grimaced at the pain. Regardless, their legs still touched, and their arms, and everything else too.

She apologized, but couldn't be sure if he deserved that apology, or if she owed him another. He made little of it, but gave her a look she couldn't understand; and didn't want to.

Gidian pointed to the platform—or tried. "My mother's making a speech again. She's never been any good at them."

Laura shivered. "I don't like her very much."

"That's fine. Neither do I." He shrugged. "Just don't listen. It's what I always do"

Gidian's mother obscured the base of the pedestal. Unlike her, it was very tall.

::::::::::::::::::::

The messenger broke the sky in a spout of fire: first a dot before the flaring son, growing upon approach, until one could make out his wings—and for a moment Laura thought him the phoenix, but instead she saw a man, chiseled out of energy, his figure borne aloft; making descent in a slow spiral, bringing his fury and heat.

He landed on the platform behind Gidian's mother, its broad surface atop pillars larger than many men together, carved of that same immutable stone. Gidian's mother screamed and dove into the crowd. Frightened, the crowd began to flee, particularly those near the back; many others attempted to do so and failed, tightening the knot. Their scream became a moan, seeming to wave in the searing gale, to permeate and destroy.

The messenger gave no indication of offense, but rather displayed himself proudly, both wings extended, each many times his considerable height, spreading further than the temple was wide. A wave of heat ran from them, igniting the foliage so that it sprung to blazing life.

Laura was spared most the heat, but screamed regardless, her eyes pained by his very brightness: skin like molten cinders, arms, torso wings extended to the points of a star. His touch was a burning pyre, seeming to rise like smoke, her heart and tribute.

Villagers fell to frantic prayer. At Gidian's insistence (he tugged her to the ground, to prevent a show of disrespect), she knelt too, but felt as though she had fallen.

The being folded his wings to a cape, woven of flame and the semblance of ephemeral feathers, and crossed both arms before his chest. Waves shimmered his flesh like currents in the river, accenting and obscuring; the torso burned darker than coals; the face like a featureless golden mask, that might even have been a replica of the sun.

None spoke, yet Laura heard anxious movements, and partook of them herself. Gidian knelt beside her. She no longer cared if they pressed together. Soon his mother would want to say something, but Laura wished she wouldn't. The being's skin breathed like fire, stirring locutions. No one could be allowed to speak in that, not without waiting.

But someone did—not Gidian's mother, as Laura had assumed, but a boy almost (but not quite) old enough to be a man, his skin seemingly anointed in oil, beard still scraggly around his neck. “Is Jacob here?” He swiveled his eyes, pursing his lips. The being nodded, seemingly in approval. Murmurs coalesced, and those shifts become a rumble. “He's not,” said a taller man, broadly muscled in his chest, bearing thick, powerful arms. “And neither is his father.” He flexed those muscles.

The messenger nodded again, gazing upwards; molten streams stirred within him. Laura thought he might hold the pose forever, like a statue, perhaps even until Jacob returned, but he did so for only a moment, a flex swarming in great wings, trailed by crimson mist.

Laura glanced at Gidian. His face seemed much older in the painful light, captured and directed by the scratches he bore. She didn't know when this had become about he and her, or "them", as a unit, but the question she saw there was a question they asked together, and she wasn't sure if she ought to resent it. Though she might.

::::::::::::::::::::

"We need to find him," Gidian said. "I suppose that's obvious."

Villagers streamed, seeking weapons.

"He isn't worth it."

"That's not what I mean." Gidian ran a hand through his hair—it shocked her even now, remembering that he looked nothing like himself. "If he leaves, if they get rid of him, he might take other things along with him, things that we need; so before he goes, if we can, we need to get those things back. If we can help him, we should do that too, but just maybe."

"I think I hate him. He's so inconsiderate."

"That's fine."

"He's never done anything for us. He wouldn't do this especially."

She sighed. A young man nearly collided with her. Night fell into a patchwork of skies. The closeness of the sun startled her, yet she felt no heaviness at its nearing departure, or very little.

"I don't like it," she said, "but we could go to his house. I doubt we'll find his father, so it doesn't matter. There isn't anything else we can do—but even if we could, how could we help him, and where would he go?"

"I don't want to look for him either," Gidian said, "and we don't have to, if we don't want. Later we might change our minds; and if we find him somewhere, we can decide what to do then. While we're doing it I could sing you a song. I'm still no good with my instrument, but I could do that for you."

"When you sing you go somewhere else, and I'd be lonely. So no, don't."

Laura stared at the ground as she walked, a subconscious gesture beyond mention, that she had done often, so frequently, but hardly thought to consider. Their feet were much the same size, even when she wore sandals. Gidian always wore large clothes, but beneath them, even if he attempted to hide it, he had the frame of a young girl. His height had ceased to matter.

"I learned to pray today," he said. "At the time I didn't know what I was doing, but I prayed for a moment."

"Were you afraid?"

"I didn't think so, but yes. I never learned how, so even if the Sun God listened, I don't think he would care very much."

"If he cares enough to watch," Laura said, "then he probably listens too, because he has really good hearing."

"He might be angry because we never pay much attention to him anymore."

"If he was, he would have told us. He told us about Jacob, at least."

"In the past," Gidian said, "they believed in him more, and he spoke to them. Maybe he told them a long time ago, but we've forgotten that also. I went there once, and met a girl who believed in him." Their path climbed a hill. "If you wanted, we could go where I met her. It's not far, and you've been there before."

"That's fine, I'd like to see. We might find something, and if not, that's fine too." They walked for a while in silence. She thought of holding his hand, or kissing him, or pushing him into the bushes, but none of those were good ideas. "Did you know your parents were going to make a child?" she asked. "I didn't know it could still be done."

"They're going to try, but it's not going to work. It doesn't work for anyone else."

"Doesn't it make you feel strange? Or angry."

"My parents were happier before I came. All they wanted was someone who had the same color hair—and later, someone to play at their meetings. When I wouldn't, I don't think they could ever love me."

"How did they do it?"

"Before, you had to petition the Sun God for a child, but for a long time he never gave his permission, and then when he stopped talking to us we stopped doing it. That's why there's less of us now."

"Sometimes I forget." Her head fell, and fell, and she added, though she hadn't meant to: "I forget lots of things." They turned another corner. Gidian stopped.

"Is this it?"

"Yes."

"Before, I'd forgotten, but I think I left something here before you walked me home."

He nodded. "I tried to find it for you, but I couldn't. It wasn't there for me."

The clearing glittered unreasonably bright. She squinted.

"In my dream," he pointed, "the lamp was right over there, by her ankle. But when I tried to get it back, I moved it, and I'm not sure where it is now. Over there," by the piled stones, "is where I slept, but it wasn't there before either. Do you see anything?"

"There!" She stepped forward. "It's by where I left it, not where you slept." Reaching the spot—without grasses, it still bore faint marks of her curves, albeit stepped upon—she lifted it. "I remember taking it with me, though."

She examined the small black container but held it from herself, fearing it would be cold, and if she touched it she might freeze also. "It isn't mine, I should have told you. Jacob gave it to me to keep, but I don't want it, so I'll give back. If he doesn't want it, then I'll give it to his father. That's who it really belongs to, anyway."

"I thought the priest followed all the old doctrines." Gidian looked closely, reached out as though to touch it, but faltered. "It isn't a real lamp, either, and that makes it worse."

Laura thought of letting him examine it himself, but didn't. "Once, when Jacob and I were out, Jacob got home after the sun rose, and his father beat him. So yes, he does, but I guess he breaks them sometimes too."

Gidian fell backwards—or up, she couldn't tell.

"There's another sun," he said. "I think I told you. If you stay out long enough, and you know how to watch, you can see it. I've never seen it rise, but it sets right before dawn. Even though it looks different, it's still about the same size—so that's a stupid tradition, because the Sun God can see us at night too."

Laura walked in front of him, still carrying the lamp. She held it as though to illuminate some invisible darkness; while unlit, it might even have done so. Its light fell upon groups searching for Jacob, and also a niche in which Gidian remembered lovers. But they were no longer there.

"We shouldn't go this way," he said. "There's a hole." But Laura insisted, and he persisted in tune. "It's deep, and you might drop it." Though he relented when he saw movement off the side of the road; and whatever had created it. Really he shouldn't have, should in fact have done the opposite, but time had made him weaker than he remembered. There was no use denying it.

Still, Laura's smile was almost endearing.

She did have a nice one.

"It's not like you think," he told her. "There are bones at the bottom. The hole doesn't look deep—with both of us, you'd think we'd be able to lift our way out—but that isn't true, because inside it would be too tall. I hate to be selfish, but I'm worried about myself just as much—no, more—than I am about you."

She said, "I don't see it."

He followed her hips as they walked. They reminded him of another reason he shouldn't have let her lead.

"The edges are covered a little. It doesn't seem like they should be, or could be, but they are." Many footsteps. "If we're going to the walls, we should take a different route. If you're coming to see the hole, you might fall. If you turned off now we might be okay, but not if that's what you're coming for."

He looked beside the road, and thought he saw it again. "This place is dangerous," he said, one last time. "We shouldn't be here." But she listened less and less, if she'd ever listened at all, and he didn't know why he followed. If he'd had any sense—if he'd been himself—he would have abandoned her, even if she did look like Sarah.

"Slow down," he repeated. "At that pace you don't even have a chance."

::::::::::::::::::::

When she fell—and she did fall—he lunged to capture her arm, her wrist (both seemed impossible slippery and smooth), but couldn't be sure he'd succeeded, all sensation drowned in her simultaneous direction, and perhaps the sensation of falling together, over and down into that abyss at the bottom, so deep that they might fall forever; but if they did hit that bottom, and if they did so together, they would stay there onto death by hunger or thirst or both—perhaps a very long time—making love occasionally, as two others as done once before, in a time beyond memory: and before or after, whether or not he fell, in the deep world, he saw something beyond a secret, that Laura herself had not seen (was incapable of seeing, because she was herself) and that he could never tell her, no matter how much she deserved to know.

::::::::::::::::::::

In the bushes at their backs, something rustled.

::::::::::::::::::::

"Should we stop here?" Laura gestured with the object, coal black and illusive. "I knew we shouldn't have gone to the walls, because he wouldn't leave it open, not now." She indicated an area between places, a children's path, masked by browning thrush but with grass beaten down behind.

Gidian shook his head. "They're sure to be searched, if there are any children with the hunters. He wouldn't be hiding there, not if he still knows how to think, and if he is he doesn't deserve to be looked for." At that, she almost seemed to sulk, and he wondered where the path had led; at where she would lead him.

They thought of another place, but Jacob wouldn't be hiding there, either.

::::::::::::::::::::::

"Would you like to come in?" Laura opened the door. She stood in semi-darkness. "Michelle isn't here yet, and when I stay here alone in the evenings it makes me sad, sometimes."

He saw she lied—evening didn't sadden her. She feared it.

She shut the door, and he discovered she possessed exceedingly comfortable furniture, more so than anything in his house, even. The couch stood before a large, proud fireplace; as of present, unlit. Michelle had slept here the night before, and if he'd heard correctly, she did so almost every night. The thought comforted him somehow, but something else too, that he found almost frightening.

"Where are your parents?" he asked.

"They aren't here," Laura said. "It used to be that they were always gone, but now they're never coming back."

"Do you miss them?"

"Not really. Sometimes I forget I haven't always belonged to them. They're disgusting."

"When I was young," Gidian said, "I used to love mine." He couldn't imagine that now. "I wouldn't mind if they did that—went away and never came back. They're trying to replace me." And later: "They're so petty."

Laura made no imprint on the cushion she sat upon: weightless. She clutched a pillow and rocked, shutting her eyes, leaning precariously backwards. She said nothing (he'd hoped she might, because somewhere inside a piece of him had fallen off a shelf, and a word from her might return it there) for an almost frightening period, until she laid the pillow down, forgotten.

"We never went to Jacob's house." She rebuked the ceiling. "I know we said we wouldn't, but we went other places we said we wouldn't, and there we might have found his father. He wouldn't have helped us either, but finding him might have helped anyway, I think."

She added: "Would it be alright if I lit a fire."

"This is your house. You don't have to ask permission.

"I wasn't sure I wanted to, but it's getting dark, and it's too quiet." She tossed on sticks and heavily burning leaves, with a tendency to the second. Those flared, and flame sputtered.

She drifted past him, flickered upon, and he followed her without moving. Haze hung about her; she glowed.

Something changed. He heard a soft crash.

"Are you alright?"

"It's the boards." Her voice lurched; what he heard there scared him. "One's broken, or it moved so I can see past it."

He rose, turned, and saw her fallen forward, dress splayed around her legs, one arm shaking against the ground. In the other she held a long thin pane.

A ripple. He shook.

"There's a light," she said, "except there shouldn't be, because there's nothing down there." Her heavy exhalations. "At least I thought there wasn't. Really."

He froze.

From the looks of it, so had she—but only one of them teetered.

"Could you help me?" she asked. "My legs aren't working right. I'm trying to move them, but they won't go. Really."

He led her backward by the wrist, at which she lunged, and he barely caught her.

Her breath:

"I should have known," she said. "You're house is like mine, but the boards don't make a sound."

And again:

"I should have known."

"We'll have to cross to get out," he said. "Is that alright?"

"Whatever you do," she said, "don't jump."

The hole was barely the thicker than his hand, but he didn't want to either. "It feels solid here. If we go around the other side, we should be able to reach the kitchen, and if we need we can leave through a window. Are you ready?"

She nodded, and he led—but though the planks seemed to waver beneath her (twice she nearly fell, and they moved, even if it might have been his imagination, or Laura herself), he never felt a thing.

"Are you alright?" he asked. She looked about to vomit, but said yes.

"It shouldn't be like that," she said. "Last night it wasn't. I made sure."

And then: "It shouldn't be like that."

Gidian began to reply, but paused.

"What is it?" she asked.

::::::::::::::::::

Deep down in his heart of hearts, like a cypher in that clear piece of crystal, Gidian had always held an image of himself carrying a large sword. In his youth, occasionally, he thought it had been handed to him. But later he realized it never had.

::::::::::::::::::

Gidian's steps were heavy in the stairway, his breath even heavier. At his side, someone else seemed to float. Before he remembered that he couldn't see her.

"We should have brought the lamp," he said. And wondered: would he have been able? (and did he want to?)

The shroud rustled. "It wouldn't light, and I'm not sure where it's at."

"You lost it again?"
"No, but it's not there anymore."

::::::::::::::::::::

A blotch of light hovered before them—he hadn't been aware the stairway turned, but it must. The steps elongated to broad platforms with no apparent boundary. The blotch seemed close, but they walked a very long way.

Though not forever. Gidian touched it: hard and smooth, like a wall. Laura traced a silhouette beside his own (he saw her in dim outline), and they pushed together—not through a door, as he expected, but a gateway, passing a surface that felt solid, but wasn't. It shut behind them, but they hadn't made it do so. He didn't think he'd opened it, either.

A fire burned in a large basin, dim and heavy. Walls ran upwards, disappearing. He looked closely for a familiar room, but saw nothing. Behind him was a picture of a door; it felt like solid stone, and even had a painted handle. An open cage sat beside it.

By the far wall, nearly invisible, something huddled. Laura's hand disappeared; he didn't know when he'd taken it. She became outline and movement.

The huddling object hardly existed, and didn't, its core an icy spike in vacant castles, haunting a frozen shore where the tides never came, playing host to a family of specters.

Or only one.

Jacob's father wiped clean the surface of his table, that had been clean many wipes ago, and if he wiped much longer, and so furiously, the sheen would go from it. If he chose, he might set a book there, a broad volume he hadn't read in whole ages; or even, by some miracle, one he hadn't read at all.

His shadow fell upon various objects without markings, its clear passage like soft, virulent smoke. His cloak, as always, fell wide and black without shadow, clasped in front, as always, and impossibly dark, as always. For whole lifetimes none had seen him without it.

Upon that flat surface, instead of a book, he laid a thin container and stone for grinding. He coughed. Jacob had taken his lantern, so he worked in seeming darkness, wide-knobbed fingers separating the herbs, measuring them, finally mixing them into dark liquid.

This he drank, and wanted to spit the sick mess—but it fell, as it had always fallen, down his crisped throat to the polluted gunk within—tightly clasping the bottle. In the past he had broken many, despite the irreplaceable glass. Many times the shards cut his palm, or fell onto his face.

Late light mixed into dust and floorboards. Setting down the beaker, he coughed once more, and began to wipe.

::::::::::::::::::::

Gidian's mother saw herself in pale outline, reflected on old, flat metal, fussing with the persistent poof of her hair. She would give anything, she thought, to make it flatter, but succeeded only by washing it in the river—and afterwards, it tended to bloat. In her youth she'd been attractive without ever approaching beauty. Someday, with the Sun God's blessing, she hoped to be young again. Her pettiness, her uselessness: how did they please him?—but even if she might forget afterwards, as they all did, she wanted to be young again.

She turned to her husband, and asked if he'd heard anything, even if she'd asked only moments before. His lips creased downwards into a frown. She knew him better than the village; knew that inside, like her, he was little but silent ash, impersonating himself. In the past, he claimed, though he forgot too, as they all did, he'd been young perhaps two or three times, but like her, with her, together, they would grow even older, and they would have no more children—no one could have children anymore—and together they would die, forgotten immediately by their son, himself older than both of them put together.

::::::::::::::::::::

Jacob fell down the walls—he'd expected a pathway, but found no indication of one—slipping quickly past the roaring glades, the recumbent mountains. He landed on his shoulder, feeling he'd broken it, in much the same angle he'd known as a child.

Immobile, he shifted his arms, his legs. He didn't have nearly the strength to lift himself. He tried, and a spike jabbed the socket. That spike represented only a part of his pain, the gentle one. Vacated of breath, he fell, eating harsh stones.

Circumventing thought, he seemed to float in a series of crimson clouds: he thought them separate from reality, but they were merely beside it. If this was a dream, he had also come here in one. Long ago, he'd lost the ability to distinguish between them.

He crawled towards a cloud—the pain impeded him, and one side of his body proved useless—to settle within it, vision obscured by chemical mists, suspended in a container. Perhaps he'd also crawled beneath a bush, or even a tree. He might never wake, but he cared nothing about that.

In sleep, something wove about him, yet he felt nothing, saw nothing, knew nothing. That thing curled in and around him, refolding and relocating, making smoother… he tossed once, but felt nothing, swirled in anesthetic dreams along a river made of song, his heart gleaming on a silent pedestal, soul eroded by deep caverns.

A cloaked man stood above him (a cloak much like his father's, but it couldn't be; he wasn't sure it was a man, either). The man wore a mask, glowing turquoise blue—or Jacob thought it was a mask, slitted thinly for the eyes; but it might have been naked skin, the rest obscured by his full cloak, and Jacob didn't see a neck, either.

The figure sowed a great needle that flared many colors, cut of prism. It entered painlessly, exited painlessly. At each suture, Jacob became looser, or tighter, until gradually he forgot original feeling; the thing replacing it felt extraordinarily familiar, as if he were reliving something that had happened to him outside, or even before he'd gone.

Perception surged redly, carrying him ever further from pain.

::::::::::::::::::

The villagers carried torches, each a fold of waxed cloth containing a piece of wood surrounded by leaves, tied off so that only the end burned, and burned slowly. Early night proved calm, but they tore past that, waving implements, prongs still streaked with dirt from their usage. They shouted. In such large groups, one might make out the sound of their footsteps from far away, seeing their torches.

At the back of one group, a small girl walked beside her brother. Occasionally, he dragged her. Her father and a small group of other men led the way, turning quickly down corners and poking bushes with pitchforks. Two smoked cigars. Imitating the men, her brother brandished a spiked implement so old, used so often, as were all such tools, as to be almost indistinguishable from the wooden handle.

She'd been present at the ceremony, also with her father and brother, but since then she'd been walking. Many days she might have gone further, but never without stopping to rest—and she didn't like the dark, that fell evilly about them, turning her father's face to that of a devil, making frightful the hoots and anger.

Her brother wore no shirt. His tan resembled dark paint, or a coat of mud. Sweat had dried by his temples, streaking the figures in his face; his torso was lean and muscular, but not yet the muscle of a grown man. The weapon looked much too big for him—certainly taller.

It had been his idea for her to come, and his idea that she remain. Most of the women had gone home; if her father had been wed, her mother would have gone also. Long ago, the girl had begun to tire, and it felt she shuffled, falling at random against obstacles, her body grown heavy.

Her brother attempted to stay with group. But once, passing a certain shrub, he gestured to her. "Come," he said, "the men won't think to go this way; they've forgotten all the old places. But Jacob might be hiding here—and if so, we could be the ones to find him."

The girl didn't want to, but she followed. She recognized the path behind the opening, layered in footprints. Stray foliage tickled her arms. Her brother moved much quicker than she did—following the silhouette of his naked torso—but he waited for her at the exit.

"Let's turn around," she said. "The men will search this area soon—the path they're on right now leads to the wasteland, and after they follow the edge for a while it comes around this way—and whatever we find, it would be better not to find it alone. If we don't go back soon, we might miss them entirely."

"If we go the opposite direction," he argued, "we could meet up with them. Father might be impressed." He brandished his weapon, leaning on it.

She shook her head. "If they realize we've gone, they'll trace the path backwards, and it will take us longer to go around. If they reach a turn, they might choose a different path than we would; and father would be angry we'd crept away. Worse, if we see them in the wastelands, because things are different there, they might not recognize us."

They continued, each repeating exactly the same argument.

"Let me check, and we can leave. I'll let you hold this," he thrust the torch at her; it burned brightly, half the length remaining, "so I can't go far." She did, until he disappeared beyond the light; yet still heard him in motion, a rustle in the leaves.

"There's nothing," he said. "Let's go."

She bent back upon the path: as she ran, following the torch against the brush (swipe and wave). Yet halfway through, she realized her footsteps were alone.

She stopped, that the boy retake her—he must have fallen, having always been a faster running than she, and he ought to do so in the moment—but he didn't appear.

The path, framed in dry leaves, took on the properties of spikes, or fangs.

She followed it all the way back, still finding nothing. He must be playing a trick on her, she thought, and resolved to hurt him for it. Yet she heard no laughter, and he wouldn't abandon her entirely, not after suggesting she follow—and nothing moved: except, a few paces beyond the edge of the pathway, she discovered something beyond mention.

She'd been correct. Noticing their absence, her father had led the party backwards, and she discovered them (by their torches, and their shouts) from a certain distance away, having already passed the entrance. She ran to him. For a moment he looked angry enough to strike her, but at her tears the anger fell away, and he asked what had happened.

She couldn't say her brother had fallen, so she said she didn't know.

::::::::::::::::::

Something moved in the space beside pathways.

::::::::::::::::::

Laura's mother turned her head. It was thin, in profile, and her outline glowed white. Laura's father, similarly, gave his blessing (unholy) in a pendulum of grease, his stature falling away to a bridge of collapsing stones.

Over them a white window arched. Both wore masks, but something showed through; excepting that, they were naked, frames warped unearthly in profile, obscured in the light from the window.

"She was right," they synchronized. "We're never coming back."

"What are you doing here?"

Jacob didn't reply. The cave appeared much the same, but not entirely so. Depending on Jacob's mood, Laura suspected it differed slightly at all times—and she felt obliged to punish him for that abscess he'd brought her, that he'd hidden in this place; or at least shine light in it.

She replaced her original question with: "Why did you bring us here?" and he didn't answer that either, yet shifted a little. The fire turned his eyes to cool silver, like the bottom of an empty bowl. Carvings hung at his shoulder, maybe a story, even accompanied by pictures, but she lacked the ability to read them.

Gidian went to the far corner of the room, and spoke to her from there, stretched across a narrow beam. "What is this place?"

"It's Jacob's," she said. "I'm not sure how, but it is. Before, I thought these objects came from somewhere, but I was wrong. I doubt they're accurate, but they're from his imagination, of the world outside the walls. Nothing of his has ever worked very well. He hides them here so they won't belong to anyone else."

She picked up a carving: small, bearing the image of some creature. "Except, now that he has them here, I'm not sure they belong to him either."

"They belong to the Sun God?"

"There's an image of him here too," she pointed, "up there. The last time I was here, Jacob spoke to him. He must have gotten permission to create this place, somehow; and he might have gotten permission to leave the valley also, but that's different, and I don't think so. Before, I left through the door we used to enter. It leads to different places because it goes behind everything. I think he must have left something there, and when I left he wanted me to take something with me. I didn't know that's what the stairway was, or I wouldn't have let us come through. Part of us might still be there now."

She considered slapping Jacob, or hurting him, or killing him, but did none of those things, because she'd already made her choice. Instead, though it was unnecessary, she gave him his warning.

"I don't think anyone can get in here unless you want them to," she said. "Get rid of the entrance, so no one can get inside." But he didn't. "You haven't gone somewhere else, have you? If you can, bring yourself back. I told you. It's dangerous."

Perhaps he understood, but no indication was given.

She stood.

"I don't want to go out through the door again," she said, "so put the entrance where no one will find it. We'll do our best to help you, but we can't promise anything. You aren't worth the effort."

::::::::::::::::

They covered the entrance with shrubs and dead grasses—too small for a man, too dark to explore—but not well. A keen eye might spot it, the clumsy might stumble into it. But having come this far, they had left that place behind.

The night felt very cool.

"Why didn't Jacob just get rid of this?" Gidian asked. "Then we wouldn't have to cover it at all."

Laura barely saw him. "I'm not sure, but I don't think he can. There has to be an entrance, or else maybe he can't get out, or the cave isn't there anymore. He can move the entrance, but not get rid of it entirely. Before, he just used himself, and moved the entrance to the wastelands at night, where no one would find it. I don't think he chose to be there. Something went wrong, or won't let him."

"If you want," Gidian said, "we could go to my house. Or I think it's mine, even if I never finished it. I built it for a girl, but she isn't here anymore, and I still have the house. It's not much, but it's mine. I'm not sure if you've been there. I think you have."

"I found it after you stole my dress," she said. "If I could, I would have killed you. But you had a hammer, and there wasn't anything else to use except a board, and that wouldn't work well enough. Say sorry for taking my dress." He did. "I'm over it now—I wore it for a while longer, until I ruined it—but it was still my favorite, and you didn't have any right to take it."

"We don't have to go there if you don't want. I didn't mean anything by it."

"Who was she?" Laura asked. "Sarah, I mean."

He took a deep breath—saying nothing.

The night was drowning, slowly but deliberately. "I've seen the sun set before," she said, "but it's better to come out earlier, when the colors are here. It's very beautiful. Sometimes I forget that."

"If we stay out longer," Gidian said, "soon the other sun will rise. If I could, I would describe it, but I'd rather not. In some ways, it can be beautiful; in others, not. If I can, I'd like to go somewhere else. I don't feel safe at night anymore."

"We can go back to my house."

"Is it alright if we move quickly?" he asked. Laura could tell from his intonation that he glanced upwards. "I'd like to get inside before it happens. We don't have very long."

::::::::::::::::::::::

"The stairs are gone," Gidian said.

"I thought they would be," Laura said. "I had a dream about them before, that came from Jacob. In it, they were there, but there was something else too, and I don't know anything about that. It's the other thing I wonder about."

He added: "Earlier, there was no reason to worry. Even if you'd fallen, and I'd fallen with you, we still would have gone to the same place. Just we might have gotten more bruises, or sprained something."

Laura shook her head. "I thought so too, but when we were down there I looked, and I didn't see anything. He wouldn't move the entrance so quickly, especially if we still needed to leave. It would have been safer for him—not us though, definitely not—if we'd used the door again, and gone back here. I don't think it led the same place at all.

"We haven't been gone very long. The fire's still burning."

"But lower." She stopped where the lost board had been; was again. "I think I used too much wood. I don't mind, because it's what people have always done—but they used it for houses, and houses last forever."

"Sometimes people forget that the trees have seeds," he said, "but they do, only no one takes care of them. You could grow your own in the garden, or even start another somewhere. Then you could trade your wood for things, just like you do with flowers."

"Maybe," Laura said. "Trees start out small, like other plants, but when they get older they get bigger too, and I don't know if I could sustain that."

"Would it be dangerous?"

"I'm not sure. Probably."

Gidian moved as though to grasp her arm; reconsidered.

"Would you mind," he asked, "if I stayed here tonight?" He looked past her at the window, grimacing; though knowing she'd see nothing, she turned regardless: and saw nothing. "My parents won't mind because they're who they are, and yours are never coming home. I'd understand if you wanted me to leave, but I won't be any trouble."

"Why?"

"I don't want to be outside in that. It scares me."

Laura studied things other than him, and wondered if they distracted her.

“If you'd asked me a few days ago, I might have said no. I won't, but make sure I don't regret it. Does that make sense?”

“Yes.”

“I was trying to figure out what made you different, but I really can't. I thought it was something that happened after you lost your instrument, but now you've got it back, and you're different again, but still alright.”

“Thank you,” Gidian said. “I might not have been able to go.”

“Would you have tried, if I told you to?”

“Maybe, but not very hard. Instead, I might have come back in later, hoping you didn't see me. If you did, I would have apologized, left, and tried again.”

“I've always known not to trust you.”

“This isn't just about being afraid, even if lots of it is. There are people out still, and I don't want them to find me. In the different light, they might think I was someone else.

“But wouldn't you look the same, because you're still yourself?

“The light hits me different because part of me is somewhere else, in a place beside things, or below them. They might see that along with me, and I'm not sure what I would look like.

“If you want,” Laura said, “we could go outside, or you could stand by the window, and I could tell you what I saw. Even if everything looked the same, you could still stay, but then you wouldn't have to be afraid.”

“I can't.” Another glance toward the window. “It's not that I don't want you to see, but I don't know what might happen. The light moves backwards, and it might take that other part of me with it. When that goes, it might take me with it, too.”

She nodded.

“I wouldn't want you to think that's who I am,” he said. “Depending on what happened, I might never come back.”

Gidian left himself at the bottom of a deep hole, or he found himself there. He stood upon lush carpet, in the chamber of a woman. Golden things and furniture: a starry array about the edges. A platter bearing food stood upon one, but it didn't look like any food he'd ever seen; and anyway, he wasn't hungry.

In the room also stood a woman with painted skin and black hair. Her white uniform clung to her, at harmony with paleness. Dark patterns swirled, whirled, and fell from her. In an unnatural way, she might have been beautiful, but she couldn't be the patroness here, she didn't have the aura. More, she seemed like a painting not content to remain on the wall... and yes, she fled from that frame, manifested (reflected) in many places at once. She stood quite close to him, so that he made out her dark lips. Yet she wasn't there at all.

Gidian put his weight on the bed, the only thing that held him. Though artfully rendered, the woman took special care to face him, less he see a sheet infinitely thin (see nothing). She sang to him: and might have been more than one woman, or even a group of them, who only looked the same, and sounded the same, and acted so similarly that they might have been (but weren't) identical.

The song was just as good—no, better—without him.

A light shone; a door opened. He followed the sound and saw no door, but an extremely tall woman, her tresses lifted to sculpted apertures, her dress a heavy, heavy purple. Despite her beauty, she seemed very old, extremely so.

"You've arrived," she said.

"I didn't know I was coming, but yes, I have."

"We don't have long, and we must be quick. Remember that you will never see me again; also that I have little to tell, and will tell you nothing if I have the option." She stripped. Though she hid it skillfully, she to existed in only two parts, as did this room. Perhaps he recognized it, also, from that place of Jacob's, his den of secrets.

She came forward, and he thought she meant to remove his clothes also; but her grip reached through that, into a place he hadn't been aware he had, and took off something else instead. Awake, he might regain it, but when he turned to see what he'd lost, she touched his face again, replacing his direction with her own; and he wondered then, if he looked into a mirror (of course the room had none), at whom he might have seen.

:::::::::::::::::

A pillow hit him in the face, and laughter, and then Laura bending over him, wide eyes impossibly colorful in the wicked brightness.

"Are you awake?" she said.

Gidian tossed that pillow back at her, rolled over, and hid beneath the blanket. His exposed back felt very cold. "I hadn't thought so. If this weren't your house, and I didn't owe you, I would probably be angry."

She giggled. She hadn't done so in a long while. Not like this.

"With you asleep," she said, "I got bored. If you'd been somewhere else, I wouldn't have been, but since you were, I was."

"I hate you."

"I thought the floor might wake you up—I walked really loud, to see if it would. It never works with Michelle either. But I thought you got up almost as early as I did." There was something he ought to remember—history and experience mulled in him—and he saw it, or felt it, but an elusive movement took it back, and he found only a dense weight, of nothing.

"Sometimes I do," he said, "but only when I sleep outside. No matter how long you stay awake, when the light hits you, it's impossible to sleep."

"Let's go find breakfast." Despite his earlier denial (in sleep), when she took a step, he *could* hear the floor. "We never ate last night."

Gidian rubbed his eyes. "I just woke up."

"If you don't come, I'll leave you. I won't bring you anything, either."

"I can't," he said, "it's too bright," and discovered, leaving, just how right he had been. Flowers writhed in their openness, scoured by light.

One had no place without the other.

Laura chose a fruit he'd never seen before. It looked funny. He wasn't sure he wanted to eat it, but it tasted surprisingly good. He asked its name, but she didn't know either, and he wondered at other places it might grow (if any) and who else had eaten it; or if they were the first.

"If you want," Laura said, "we can go back to your house." (He knew the one she meant.) "I don't mind now, during the day, but at night it would have been scary."

Gidian shook. "We can't." And stared at his hand. A lump stuck in his throat, impossible to swallow, bobbing. "I'm not sure why I suggested it. There's nothing left, and it isn't even haunted."

"You don't miss it?"

"—I have to go." He finished the fruit all in a quick bite, stood, and pretended to dust himself. "I'll take you there later, if I can, but there's something I have to think about first."

She said nothing.

"I hope you not angry at me, after you let me sleep in your house. I really do appreciate it."

"I don't understand," she said, "but I don't understand anything anymore, so just go."

"I was right." He touched the brim of his hat. "You sound angry."

"I'm not, just confused." She turned her head. "I'll find you later. I always do."

Gidian left, but he had forgotten where he was going. Decision, a shifting pressure, wavered within his grasping space, and would not leave it.

Passing villagers, he asked about Jacob. Who had yet to be found. Gidian, bearer of secrets, wondered if he ought to divulge them. For there was fear in their voices. Next to that, Jacob didn't, and had never mattered. They owed him nothing.

The shack—Laura referred to it as a house, but it had never been anything like that—looked just as desolate as he remembered. He stood against the tree. Unused boards piled on its far side, and the walls had collapsed. Beside the hole, another had detached entirely.

Moving to the door, he saw the stains within. It still bore the marks of his body, much writhing, and evil sleep. He remembered something of a dark presence, but very little. Beneath that spot, part—no, most—of him might still be there, despite being in innumerable others also.

A rustle at his back, and a soft voice.

"I thought I might find you here." Laura said.

He turned. "I knew you would follow me. I'm glad you did." He paused. "But there isn't anything here anymore, and there never was."

And then: "After I broke my instrument, you came here, right?"

"Yes."

"I saw you. You were very bright with the light behind you, and I didn't know what you were."

"I remember."

"You never came inside, but before you left you said something. Ever since, I've been wanting to ask you what it was, but I always forget."

"I don't think I said anything at all."

"You must have—unless it was something I wanted to say to *you*."

"Who was she? Sarah, I mean."

"She was you," Gidian said, "or she looked like you. I wrote a song about you once. When that song came to life, I realized how much of myself was in it, and everything else. Then I put more. I'm not sure why it was that song, because I'd worked on others just as hard, or harder. But even when the words were different, they were still the same. She spoke to me sometimes, in a language only I understood. She was beautiful, like you, and I loved her."

"Is she gone?"

"After I destroyed my instrument, I think so. I'm not sure."

"I think I've seen her. She looked like me, but paler. I don't think you noticed, but she looked like you too."

Adding: "She's why I found you so often, isn't she?"

"Yes."

"I ought be angry." Gidian didn't agree out loud, but she knew. "I don't belong to you like that; I never gave the permission."

"I didn't realize it was happening," he said, "until afterwards. When I did, it was already too late. But I wouldn't have stopped anyway." He took a deep breath. "You can hit me if you want, any amount of times, with whatever you choose. I might not be able to talk for a while, especially if you hit me in the mouth. I haven't been healthy recently, so there'll be lots of blood. If you break my fingers, it would make sure I never played music again."

Laura closed her eyes, considering it. (The idea was easier to suggest than the reality to bear, and he'd never dealt well with pain.... He shivered, and a cool wind seemed to blow—yet another rampant imagining. There was no tree, he remembered, and something sounded like wind, but wasn't.) She opened them.

"I couldn't," she said. "Jacob did more than that, but I'm even helping him, and so are you." He wondered at her thoughts. "Depending on what happens, I might change my mind, but unless I hurt Jacob first, I won't do anything—and even then, less seriously. But Jacob might not survive."

Exhalations escaped his clenched teeth. He thanked her, realizing his hands had been knotted to fists. "I might not sound serious, but I mean it, and if I can I'll make it up to you. At least I'll try."

"Did you love her?"

"More than I can accurately describe," he said. "If I could, I would tell you through a song, but I can't do that anymore either. If I ever remember, I'll play it for you. I realize now that others never enjoyed my music as much as I did because I was playing for myself. But this song, or at least part of it, I wrote for you."

"I don't remember the last time someone's been in love with me," she said. "It's nice."

Gidian exhaled. Particles waved in a phantom wind, and something towered above them both that looked nothing like a tree.

"If Jacob goes," Laura said, "we might get something back. It's not selfish to want that, is it?"

"I don't think so. Not with how much he owes us."

::::::::::::::::

Awakening—though, like all dreams, this one was quickly forgotten—Gidian realized that, like so many times before, that thing cast off had been himself. Still, looking into a mirror, he didn't know what he might have seen: but almost certainly, despite a vague resemblance, the face would not have been his own.

They grew light for the coming wind, spread like color across a vast, elaborate expanse: the landscape sharing its profile, from which there can be no departure, and all things are perpetually new. Exhausted from play, they formed a circle, holding hands, and exegesis took the place of roses. Soon, they would leave this place, but soon after they would come again. Jacob told of myths and legends. Gidian sang songs. Laura spoke truth about the flowers.

They watched shadows bend gradually longer, yet the sun shone even as the plains cooled. Unlike the village, one might walk all day unobstructed by the maze-like gardens; vision carried to the far off wall, or walls, that did not move, and here would never do so.

Of the three, only Jacob played often, while Laura walked amongst the flowers, and Gidian practiced his music. Their intersection took place only at certain times, a *coming together*; this too was a requirement. For these reasons they had been chosen. Certainly, it could be no other way.

In truth, Jacob was the only child among them—perhaps the last to be born in the village, and if not, nearly so. Gidian and Laura had lived many lives, and carried something, if not much, of that with them. For many reasons he did not belong among them, this being only one among many, many more.

::::::::::::::::::::

The girl accompanied her father as he searched for her brother, and the men followed, become now a party of rescue, eschewing the hunt. Had she been able to, she might have led them through the secret place, but tried and failed to find it; also, attempting to lead them around, she discovered she'd been wrong in her evaluation of the two locations, even if, then, she hadn't been. It didn't surprise her, and having been young before, her father knew of such things—but though they searched long into the morning, they found nothing, not even that thing beyond mention (her nightmare) of which she could not speak, and would never do so.

::::::::::::::::::::

Gidian's father organized a village meeting. Only half of what he'd expected came—his own wife had been unable to attend—and all looked exhausted, their beards unkempt, their boots dirty. The hall (a cramped, rather poor building to which he'd grown so accustomed) seemed somewhat empty, but charged with a frightening energy. Some had brought their children. He stood behind a makeshift podium at the head of the room. At these times, and these times only, he felt like an important, essential member of the congregation. He'd yet to shave, despite being out only a short while last night. Nor had he bathed.

Their conversation fell silent when he spoke.

"As you know," he said, "we've been charged with giving Jacob to the Sun God. The Sun God is not known for his patience. The messenger might return today, or tomorrow. For days now he has shown us the signs of his anger. In order to prevent this, we must locate him soon.

"There was much search last night, but many areas have been missed, or searched poorly. I suggest we group together and make that search methodical, blocking off any escape that Jacob might have. If he's still here, there's nowhere he could possibly hide. With a group of this size, we'll cover the entire valley before nightfall.

"Are there any objections?"

::::::::::::::::::::

Golden beams streaked the sky. Here, the sun looked more like an eye than it ever did outside: a tapering oval, outlined in lashes. They lifted upwards: luminous pulse onto a higher kind of platform. This heightened sensation defied descriptive prowess, proving that truth is mightier than language.

Jacob had a fondness for rolling down the hill. He had done so for as long as they could remember. At the hill he grew exuberant, nothing at all like himself outside. There, that missing piece, something none of them recognized, or recognized only when its place had been taken, ceased to matter, and he attained a humanity unimaginable anywhere else.

On one occasion, at the base of the hill, Jacob picked a flower and presented it to Laura. She thanked him by hitting him in the face. He'd never understood the connection between her and others; while here, she was connected to everything. No soul flitted languidly upwards, and drowned now in the palm of his stupid hand, petals in scandalous song, fading to worthless mist.

Here, like no other place in the village, when she touched that linkage between herself and the sun (like a long string, or cable; usually transparent, but here it became solid) it could actually be felt. One day, if she could bare that pain, she might climb upwards, to find discovery there—though of course she never would.

Gidian preferred silence, and such a thing they gave him. In return, they spoke into glorious music: his song melded with that of the flowers, and clarity fell as transient rain. In these moments, he proved himself sensitive and human, no matter that he would deny it. He spoke in a voice made of sunlight, enraptured by the plains.

Everyday they came here, erasing past lives, forever altering those to come. A part of it they would carry with them always, in exchange for something else. None knew if they would be reborn—certainly, Jacob wouldn't—but even if they were, having come here, having been cleansed, they might not remember. Was it worth all that? Yes, very probably it was.

::::::::::::::::::::

Jacob stood at the center of a large, hollow chamber. Light hung about the rafters, yet none fell to him: it seemed he fell perpetually. He feared to take a step lest he be atop a thin black pillar, and in taking that step, be removed. Gleaming quietly, two eyes looked down from the ceiling, seeing all the way through him.

::::::::::::::::::::

Jacob's father saw a mirror on one wall—unbelievably old, he feared looking there, lest the substance shatter. Yet he did so now, and polished it: large yellow eyes, hinged red, the pupils swollen, set into his broad, wrinkled forehead; the grand archipelago of his nose, broken by two wide canyons (his nostrils) and clogged with thick gray hair.

He heard another knock on the door. Ignored it. He'd talked to two, perhaps three searchers by now, whom had tired him more than usual—and when they refused to leave (perhaps under the impression he'd hidden Jacob in a cupboard), he'd contemplated attacking them.

Fastening his cloak tightly about his shoulders, he fetched his long staff—he had difficulty going about without it—and a second, older lamp that he'd hidden. This was much larger than the one Jacob had taken: cleaner, smoother, without defect. He refrained from igniting it, of course; in the remaining day, there was no need. Yet the light moved quickly, and subtle strings unraveled in him.

::::::::::::::::::::

It is impossible to know the valley without having been there. Despite the variety of landmarks within, one thinks only of the sun, walls, and gardens. But there is much here beside those, and one must offer them attention occasionally. For life here is a compendium of these exceptions.

Most trails end at the wasteland. Very few take them, but in a sense there is only one trail, all connected by filament and web. Some say it is possible to travel them all without ever overlapping, but this statement remains unproven. The paths themselves are of either dirt or grass.

In the distance one sees the walls. Nearer, their motion becomes apparent, but from far away they resemble black lines upon the wide, circular horizon. Excepting the hill in the center of the valley, it is impossible to see all the walls from one point, as vision is obstructed by the sloping terrain or the temple itself.

Beside the path, one finds items of every imaginable shade. Sharp leaves, glittering gold, become a varnished wall of hanging features, dotted with blossoms. Behind this lies a tangle of stems and thorns, but occasionally one locates a hidden pathway. Between even these, in the places no one has ever gone, where the garden has grown over entirely, are the ruins of older stone monuments, unseen for eons.

—But no, this account says nothing about life there, and it isn't worth the time.

That evening, the messenger approached. Again, he wore moisture, and his hair stuck to his scalp. He'd fallen once or twice. Inhalation: he shook, and spoke as though vomiting, in pangs.

"Oh," Gidian said, and looked as though he wanted to say more, but fell silent.

"Who has him?" Laura asked. "And do you know where?"

"I'm not sure, but he's been seen with his father." The messenger barely stood. "They were walking together, or his father was dragging him. As soon as someone saw that, I'm not sure who, they sent me out."

Choking, he knelt, wiped his forehead, and recovered some inner reserve.

They returned to the place of communication. Gidian's mother and father fussed among the crowd. Fights had broken out. Scores of men bled upon the ground, holding broken noses and jaws primarily, but one had a broken arm.

Locating a noncombatant, they asked what had happened.

"They don't know where Jacob is," the girl replied.

"Was he ever here?"

"They don't know that either." Something spiked flew over their heads. A cry of pain rang out. "A mistake might have been made concerning Jacob and his father, but it's doubtful. More likely Jacob escaped again—no one knows where exactly he's been hiding—or they did have him, and someone else took him. I'm surprised they found him at all; I thought he'd left already."

"The messenger will probably be here soon—"

"Or he's come already," the girl interrupted. She cringed; the fight continued to spread. "No one knows that either." She broke away from them and disappeared atop a hill, behind a bush, presumably to join another group of onlookers.

In a reddened sky, tinged citrus, something churned.

::::::::::::::::::

Not long afterwards, they found him themselves.

::::::::::::::::::::

The priest had taken Jacob to the old altar. A crowd, much smaller than they'd left, gathered around him, watching silently: lived in silence. Jacob had been hit repeatedly, absorbing rocks as well as fists. One, the size of a large bowl, lie next to him; its whole side glistened. Turgid currents painted his chin. More decorated his father's fists, forcefully taken; flecks splattered to directions, a hideous rain. Jacob stood only because he was made to, like a doll, on a hook, on a string. His eyes he held shut, head lolled to one side.

He groaned.

"I made this boy from myself." The father tossed him to the ground. He attempted to crawl, but a foot came down on his head; ricochet and bounce; slurp and brittle cracking. "I gave him life, and he isn't grateful. I gave him my blood, and he isn't grateful. I gave him myself, and he isn't grateful. All that, and he doesn't know a thing about gratitude." The priest removed his cloak, and the heavy fabric wavered. He wore a thin white shirt. The body beneath was twisted like a tree.

He buried his boot in Jacob's spine, and repeated the motion: a furious rise and fall… his countenance shook, spectacles unhinged, lips crushed past expression; he began to growl. The rock rose, fell, and formed a crater, that gushed. Jacob's skull, planted in the earth, shook. His father lifted him once more, continuing to shout—the words impossibly garbled—and hurled him onto the altar, scattering stones.

"He never came back!" The priest unleashed froth: a fountain. "He took so much of me—the most important part—and he never brought it back!" He punctuated each word with a blow, so spoke at a limping, earthy pace. "You see!" he exclaimed, and tore off his shirt, revealing layered bandages. These he removed also, freeing the wrinkled, eaten flesh beneath. His stomach was a gaping cavern, its edges rimmed in seeds, like the pod of a plant. That wound had never healed, and green fluid leaked from it still, a crusted stain on discarded gauze.

"The Sun God refuses to give us children," he explained, "and so I made one myself, from myself." Spread lips revealed pointed teeth. Green tones showed clear in his skin, the tinge of rotting. "He wasn't good for it," the father continued. "He wasn't good for anything." Bending (it seemed what remained of his guts might spill from the compression) he retrieved a knife from his cloak, the knife Jacob had taken from the cave. Even then, Laura had feared it.

The creature hefted Jacob and ran the edge along his cheek, painting a line. "This is the blood I gave him," he proclaimed, "and it is mine to reclaim." The gash oozed, widening.

He slit Jacob's tunic to reveal the emaciated form beneath, startlingly pale. The torso showed his ribs, useless shields about a shriveled core. Cuts decorated him here also, but primarily a family of bruises, most too old to have been inflicted today.

"There is nothing within this worthless husk!" The priest plunged the knife into Jacob's stomach. "I'll show you!"

And began to cut.

Blood surged around and beneath it, forming rivers. The blade wandered, loosely following a path, until there was nowhere else to go.

Completing the incision (thrust and pull), the priest reached within, pulling the flaps open. He drew out a black lump (nothing left in that clear piece of crystal). His narrow eyelids drew thinner, snarling.

"You see!" he shrieked. "Worthless!"

Knobby fingers crushed the stone to inky powder; carried it to the hungry mouth. The creature's tongue was long enough to wrap around the entire hand, and left an acid residue.

He belched.

And from the look he gave the body, Laura knew he would eat it, all of it, starting here, with the rotted soul, until he'd consumed it all: meat, bone, vital organs—but there was nothing left in it, or very little, and afterwards he would scream, and curse, and continue to be a monster, having proven himself one indeed.

He licked the knife, hoisting the flesh—perhaps it still lived, but doubtfully—and gazed over their heads, into the bushes. What he was waiting for, what he expected to see—beyond dreadful imaginings—never came, or hadn't come yet, and he passed the blame onto his son's face, utilizing the mighty fist: yank, crash, and the cranium shot backwards; then forwards.

Sheathing the knife in Jacob's gut, he turned the body around with both hands, holding it away from himself.

"A long time ago," he said, "there was a time when our people had wings."

And flew.

He lifted the blade, this time for a shallow, almost careful incision below one shoulder; then a duplicate beside the other; and let the weapon fall. Reaching inside, he drew out, one at a time, a pair of murky, stunted tufts, clotted black with a whole lifetime's blood.

Removing both—Jacob convulsed at each pull; dark sprays shot from him—the creature let him fall. He brought the wings to lips, to suck upon the clots. Each wing was hardly larger than Laura's hand, mottled in sticky feathers, but in the past, on someone else, maybe even herself, or Gidian, they must have been beautiful.

Finished with both, the priest bent and took hold of the body, this time by the neck, and hefted it high as it would go.

Something sprang from the bushes.

Laura saw it for only a moment, but knew it immediately—its red skin, its wretchedness, its inhumanity—as a monster that ate flowers, lurking all day within leaves and peaking out through them, its yellow eyes ringed in secrets, its breath a rustle indistinguishable from them. It soared above their heads to land before Jacob; without halt, it seemed to dive, squeezing head, arms, and shoulders past his teeth, down the throat and into his self—or where, in someone else, there might have been a place for one.

Jacob's eyes sprang open, and rolled back into his head. He shook, a methodical shaking, back and forth, like a coil of rope unwinding, or branch swinging....

Then, very loudly, he screamed: thrashing at his father and himself, the blood gushing with new fervor from his ruined shell, the feeble husk; and somewhere, the door to a cage had fallen shut, and there were no more doorways, within or outside his blasphemous darkness.

::::::::::::::::::

They'd been invisible before, but during the ceremony became clear: a series of cords, not one but many, tethered into Jacob, that led not to the sun but a place beyond the walls; and now, slithering, began to recede.

::::::::::::::::::

In a new place, Laura shivered. It was too dark for many things she knew, and an evil caricature hung above her, pendulous against void.

"That was hideous," she said. "I don't care if Jacob deserved it. And he didn't, because if he had, I would have told him."

Gidian nodded. He knew.

"What would you have done," she asked, "if you'd been Jacob's father?"

"Jacob's father was very old. Much older than both of us put together, in all of our lives. He thought different than I did, and cared about different things, so I can't say.

"But Jacob wasn't really so different from Sarah," Laura said, "except Sarah came from someone else instead of just you. You gave her the same things, and she hasn't given them back."

"If she came back," Gidian said, "then I would love her. Just like I did before."

"What if she never gave herself back?"

"That's all I gave her. If she did, she wouldn't be there anymore, and it would make me sad."

"Your parents are never going to have another child. You should tell them, in case they're in denial."

"They wouldn't listen." Gidian spat. "They never do."

Pulling ahead, she thought of others who had, crossing her hands like a shield. The walls spun wide in a circle, a disk, and the river slid upwards, its crystal towers refracting the glow.

Gidian touched her arm and she stopped.

"We shouldn't go this way." He gestured beside the pathways. "This is where it lived before, and there's no telling what we might find. And also, there's the hole. The last time we went there—remember, I caught you, or I meant to—I saw something at the bottom. We should turn around."

But again, she insisted.

They turned off the path, into a secret linkage. Within it, Gidian paused. "I saw it over there," he said, "so if we turn here, we'll find its home." He probed the bushes, parting them. She followed. The foliage fell away, become a frail display, varnished white, that crumbled at the slightest touch; that broke.

"I've been here before," she said, "but I ran."

"Are you sure you want to go further? There's nothing we'll want to see." She nodded, and they continued, igniting a particle rain, petals falling like pieces of ash—they reminded her of the old man, and she cringed. Layered waves peeled the feeble shell. She seemed to drift, to wander within a wintry dream.

They came to a place where the flowers grew shorter. Gidian paused. Before them, bleached just as white as the flowers, lie a naked skeleton, opalescent in the boughs, the clouds.

Gidian fell back. She turned, questioning.

"Michelle's never coming home," he said. "She hasn't been home for a very long time."

::::::::::::::::::::

Leaving the den of flowers, they returned to the path. Laura continued to cry. Gidian walked behind her. “We should get off this road,” he said. “We've fallen once. If we fall again, we might never get out.”

And then: “There are bones at the bottom.”

Laura cared very little. He shrugged.

::::::::::::::::::::

They fell.

Gidian inspected his hands for cuts, but saw none, despite the pain. He blinked: heightless, weightless, tired.

"We survived," he said. "That's good. I didn't think we would make it this far." He turned his head, and saw many things familiar. "If we can, we should try to get out, but I don't think we'll be able to. The hole looked shallow from above, but I'm sure you can see, it barely has a top it's so high."

Laura said nothing.

"I think I've been here before," he continued. "It was different then, because I couldn't see out, but the carpet was here, and some of the decorations. I met a woman. She said I'd never see her again, so we won't, but I must have left something."

"We could stay if you want," Laura said. "It's pretty, and there's a bed that we could sleep in until we die."

"Are you alright?"

"It feels good to be alone with you. I just thought you should know."

Gidian looked upward because it was easier that way. Despite his invitation to sit, Laura stood, and he wished she hadn't. The bed was comfortable but the blanket had a strange design on it: a crinkly gold substance that came off on his hands. It tilted in her invisible direction.

"You can't tell," he said, "or if you can I can't, and you haven't mentioned it, but this place is flat, and while we're in it we're flat too. It's why size works different from outside, and sight and images and things. Out there, all it does is pretend to have them, but in here it can't hide that anymore."

"That makes sense I suppose. It's like Jacob's doorway, except that leads everywhere, and this has no way out."

Yes, he said, that's exactly what it was.

"If we had wings we could fly." She gazed wistfully upwards, and touched her lips. "We could leave the valley whenever we wanted, and come back." Like they had power. "That would be nice," she said. "It really would."

"If I leave, do you want to come with me?"

"No." She blinked. "Maybe yes, but I don't think so."

"We can't stay here." A painted face seemed to dance before him, but it wasn't there.

"Why not?"

"There isn't anything but us, and that isn't enough. I wish it was, but you would get tired of me soon."

He didn't add that if he'd had his instrument, maybe she wouldn't have.

Laura took a deep breath.

"What?"

"Your hair," she said. "It's back."

Gidian stared at her.

"Can I touch it, just once?" She giggled, and he wanted to run—to where, he didn't know, but a cupboard might have been alright, or a closet. "I wanted to before, but I never cared enough to ask. And besides, it's never been this shiny either."

Gidian said she could, and her fingers were gentle like water.

"It's soft," she said. "Almost as soft as mine."

"Thank you."

"I wouldn't have told you that before, but I will now. Does that mean something?"

"No." He wanted to run, but not from her. There was something else, and it had been here already. "Sometimes if you take something and move it, it can be the same, but it can be different too."

"What do you mean?"

"There are bones."

"What?"

"Over there." He pointed. "Look."

"Who's are they?"

"Ours." Gidian's chin met his fingers: philosopher. "The last time we came here, part of us fell, and only a little of us was left to come back. But that doesn't explain why I still have my hair, because I didn't have it when *we* fell. So I must have fallen before, maybe more than once, without knowing it."

"I wonder how that happened."

"Me too."

"Can I sit down?"

"If you want."

"I don't." Laura spun, fallen upon by light, radiant in shadows.

"There are other people here too," he said. "There have to be, because I felt them, and when they get lost, this is where they come. We just can't see them, because they're flat too, in a different way than we are."

Laura poked a vase. Gidian hoped it might not fall.

"And I know why Jacob needed his cave," he said.

"You do?"

"Jacob was keeping this place there, except somehow it got out. I saw it in a painting—or I saw the empty frame, and it fit somehow. He had to keep things there, because if they got out they would be real like this hole, and he didn't want anyone else to have them."

"He's always been selfish," Laura said. "I knew it."

"Before, when I came here, I wasn't really dreaming, just visiting the parts I'd left behind." Gidian led her to the far side of the room, and pointed beneath a table. "And that time she took even more."

Laura shivered.

"These are our bones," he said, "or what's left of them. There are two more of me somewhere, and maybe more of you too."

"Oh," she said. "So that's where I went."

"I think they were alive before we got here, but when we fell we became them, or they were part of us. I might not be right, and they might belong to someone else, but I don't think so.

"No one else is going to get out either." Gidian stepped away, resolved never to come back, or even remember; and felt he peeled himself into layers. "Jacob was a murderer. He ate Michelle, and killed anyone that fell in here—not by actually doing it, but he let it happen, and he deserves the blame."

Gidian wanted to look away from his skeleton—it was larger than Laura's, just a little, and grinned—but he never did.

"Jacob never came back," Laura said. "I should have told you."

"How do you know?"

"Everyone has a cord that comes out of their back," she explained. "It leads to the sun, even if I can't see it right now. If we could touch them, though you can't do that *out*side either, maybe we could use them to climb. But we can't. They're still there, but not in the same way, which means they really aren't."

She reached as though to make sure. Gidian didn't do so himself, but he wanted to.

"Everyone has only one cord," she said, "and they always lead to the sun. But Jacob had four or five, and they led back over the walls."

"What does that mean?"

"When Jacob came back, he didn't bring anything with him, even himself. Something brought *him* instead."

"Do you know what they were?"

"I saw one of them once, but I didn't know it. I'd like to think it hadn't been here already, even before Jacob, even if it said it was."

"Have you ever thought," Gidian said, "that maybe Jacob never left at all?"

But it was as though he'd never asked the question.

"Won't you stay?" Laura took his arm, and her touch was gentle, and soft, and it flowered. "I've made up my mind. Even if you leave, I'm staying. But if you do, I'll be lonely."

"No," Gidian said. "It wouldn't be right, and I'd end up coming back for you anyway, when you'd changed you mind."

"You're a horrible person. I hope you know that."

"I do," Gidian said. "But only sometimes, and this isn't one of them."

Laura took her hands away, and stepped backwards. She looked like she was about to cry; Gidian considered comforting her, but he'd never understood sympathy.

She said: "I didn't mean it, what I said before."

"What?"

"I didn't really want to stay. I just thought that's what you wanted, even though you said it wasn't. But don't worry, I'm over it. Do you believe me?"

"Alright."

"You should. It's the truth." She pulled back—poised behind a golden screen, where he could barely see her.

"There's something wrong," Gidian said. "There's something here, besides the other people."

He hesitated, looking deeply into her eyes. Behind them, he saw something different."

"Sarah, are you there?"

Yes.

"I'd thought so. I couldn't feel you before, but things are different here."

I'm sorry. I know I don't have permission, but after Jacob brought her through the doorway the second time, he took so much of her that if I hadn't come back she might have died.

"Where were you, before that?"

In another place, beside this one. When I came back to her, most of me stopped being me anymore, except me. Until we came here, I wasn't there at all.

"Can you get us out of here? You can fly, I think."

I'll try. Normally I wouldn't be able to lift you, but things here are different. Will she mind?

"I hope not. But it's better she leave. Will you be there, outside?"

I don't think so. I hope.

"It was nice to talk to you. I'm glad."

::::::::::::::::::

They flew—like the rising river, a pillar of light—they flew.

::::::::::::::::::

Dusk swiveled triumphant, smoldering the skylands. Undulation: flush and downwards. Yellow lit up, painting a curtain. Gidian had watched the sun set many times, but hardly had it been like this.

A silver arc ran across her: Gidian couldn't tell, whether reflection or impression. For the first time in many days, the night made him heavy.

"Why do think religion disappeared from the valley?" Laura asked.

"Did it?"

"There are no places left for it here. Not in the things we keep."

"No matter what," Gidian said, "we still have stories. As long as we have the sun, and the walls, and the gardens, we'll still have those."

"They don't say anything."

"Until we forgot how to fly, I don't think we had a religion at all; until the valley was all we knew, and we wrote stories about it. So we didn't lose anything."

"Sometimes," Laura said, "I wish I could be a flower." She bent. "Sometimes I get memories," and swayed, "and in them I can hear the song even better than I can now." Did he know what she meant?

He nodded, hearing also.

"I told Jacob about it before," she said, "but he wasn't like you, and he couldn't. I said a lot of things Jacob didn't understand, but I don't think he understood the rest either, only pretended he could."

And flew.

"That's another reason to be a flower," she said. "I could sing."

He had a vision of which she spoke: lofted in tangerine clouds, ocean and landscape. "I could teach you, if you wanted."

"You could try—no more than I could teach you to grow flowers." She trailed off. "But if you could—grow flowers I mean, just so I know—would you?"

"It sounds nice. I've never thought of it much."

"I don't think I meant what I just said, about learning to sing, but it did sound good when I said it."

"If you want," Gidian said, "we could stay out all night, to watch the other sun rise."

"Will it come?"

"I thought it might leave with Jacob, but he wasn't big enough, and it's always been there."

And then: "I could describe it for you, like you said before. Maybe if I did you could see it."

"Maybe I could."

And swept, blurring wildly.

::::::::::::::::::::

Negative junction and he rose... perception, formerly dark, shot into hyper-alignment, shading into fundament. Descriptions came to him, but did not leave, and had nothing in common with words: his smoldered self suspended in gel-constitute, thicker than water, rippling like it... in a way, he realized (having risen, having dreamed) the whole universe was submerged under water; not water but something resembling it, that wrapped around to bring the lines. Color split without a single, unified shade—glitter torrents, heaving particles, a mixture of stars; the sun above that (he proclaimed it monster but it wasn't, just another, that moved backwards) trickled mixtures down its green and gold belly, the broadening penultimate. Bridges led to it. Dust speckled their immaterial length, spanning dimension. Gidian ascended and flew; without body or anything but himself he flew—or seemed to, but did not move very far. Beside him was someone beautiful, that he loved, and they touched their hands together (he imagined)—twining vessels onto prurient dreamscapes, a double helix: like shining light, liberating stars....

The ritual is our oldest tradition because it is also the reason for our valley: the sun and walls would grow lifeless without it. Within the temple there exists another dimension, a preserved version of the valley as it was before people came there. It contains another sun, and another valley. But perhaps it, and not ours, is the original. In either case, one acts as the foundation for the other, enacting suspension.

We are shadows.

Beneath them both (beneath all things), there is something else, another place, where light moves backwards, and all things are different. But I could also say inside, or between. That other place takes up our empty space, and we do the same in reverse. Sometimes, when I lose track of myself, I slip between the empty spaces, and I don't like it there. Together, these two are the foundations of time—or time in the linear sense, a paradox.

The universe has six layers, all of which take up the same space and have their own rules; then they have their own sub-layers, and the holes between those. Someday maybe it won't be like that anymore—one layer will take over another, making less, or somehow we'll get another—but I don't understand any of that.

The first layer is nothing. It only has one part. Nothing can exist within that, or nothing solid. Maybe something comes from there, the parts that don't really belong in other layers, that leave there when they don't have a container anymore. Wherever there is energy, something leads there, and maybe something comes out, but I'm not sure.

The second layer has two parts, like a piece of paper. They look like they have more, but they're like a mural attached to the bottom of the third layer, and they never do. At a bunch of places, you can get into it from there, or come out, but you always stay the way you were before, if you had a shape, so it doesn't work.

The third layer is where we live. Everything has three parts, enough to make them solid. The properties things have here apply everywhere, but they don't always *mean* the same things. When you look close enough, if you want, you can see dots, or blocks, or colors; and after you've looked at the pieces, you can take them apart, and examine the connection with other parts in the third layer, but there's so much you never really find anything.

The fourth layer has four parts, the fourth being time, in a nonlinear sense. In our layer, everything happens only once; whereas in the fourth, everything that has ever happened exists separately, and it's possible to move between them. Because of this, everything that ever happened has happened already, and happens again at every moment. But there is no such thing as a moment; it's hard to understand.

In the fifth layer, everything exists everywhere at once, so there's no such things as space or objects. Instead, everything moves inside everything else, like water within water—that doesn't describe it, but it's the closest I can get. There are things there (there are things *everywhere*) but they're so different from us we can't even be compared: the first point, obviously, is that they don't understand the meaning of one, as in single, as in us.

The sixth layer is everything—but in a sense, it might only be the first layer again. Nothing can exist there, because everything exists already. All energy comes from this layer, just as, when it leaves, it goes to the first. So far, it's infinite, but it doesn't leave much room for the places in-between, because next to the infinite they don't seem natural, and they might be crushed someday—and then made again.

Really there are many more (layers within layers) but for the most part those other layers are subdivisions, with subdivisions of their own, and this is the best I can describe them to myself. And all I can do is describe them loosely, like they really have "parts" that can be expressed so simply, or be expressed at all, which they don't.

Jacob's father knew most of what I just said (I learned it from his old, old books) but he knew so many other things too, and believed them all, that he couldn't be said to "know it" it any definite sense. But I don't trust my judgments either. I've thought about it a lot, but I don't know everything, so I can't say everything. At best, what I said is a little true, but not completely. I think.

Our world is very, very old. Outside, the world was *too* old, and too full of holes between layers. By taking the two images of it—the one inside the hill, and the one outside—and superimposing them on each other, we manage to get rid of that other, the dark one (or mostly, by pushing it to the side), so the valley exists somewhat outside linear time, and escapes most of its problems. The sun (it is many things, among them a gateway) brings energy from the sixth layer, to keep us going, and though the other sun appears, it takes much less than the real one gives. As long as the ritual continues, the sun will know that there are people here, and for as long as it can, it will keep working. It's necessary to maintain a connection between both valleys, to keep the other sun blocked off, or it might go away. I'm not sure why we use children, but it must be symbolic. Everything else is.

In order to keep people from disappearing, the sun puts them in containers. When a soul first appears, it's blank, but the longer it stays, the more it changes. If you die, it goes back to wherever it came from (either the first or sixth layer) and that goes away. Outside, when you died, you used to fall into the dark place, and leave from there; but here, the sun catches you before that, like a net, and you come back down, to become something else, or go into another body. It has ways of making more bodies even if it hasn't done it since before I was born.

I've never been to the sun, and so I don't know if someone lives there or not. Father thinks there isn't, and he's probably right. There isn't a *person* in there, or anything like a person; but there must be *something*, or more than one of them, that thinks, causes process. I'm just not sure what to call it.

Though I might just have lied. I've never been *to* the sun, but I think I've been through it. When father broke the instrument, or the part of himself that made it, I didn't go near it, but I went to that other place, and I stayed there for much longer this time. Before, I hadn't gone there fully, meaning part of me stayed here, and so I still knew where to go. But with no path back, I had to go through the sun instead. It frightened me, and I didn't know how. Like before, even if I used it this time, I didn't go *through*—but it propelled me, and I came out Jacob's doorway, or most of me did.

First, I wanted to see father, but now there was even less of me, and he probably wouldn't be able to. If I wanted I could have become part of Laura again (I'd like to call her mother, but I can't, because we look so much like sisters) and for a while I did, and I still might be. I never existed in an individual sense—more like I was a piece of them cut off and mixed with other things.

I made up Jacob's story, or most of it. Some of it was in his head, but not the important parts, and I couldn't go in there because it was a dangerous place, and scary. Maybe he did go those places (I'm not sure how old the world outside is, if it moves, or if there are people) but it doesn't matter: he might only have sat there for days, only feet beyond the walls. After those *things* got inside him, they planted themselves in him, and that was what I found, with him inserted—or while he sat there, he imagined it.

I've been telling this story for myself but there isn't anyone left anymore. Just me, and no others.

::::::::::::::::::

Father said nothing: he wanted to, but he didn't have the time. We rose up, and up, and up, and up. Metallic rainbows stained the silvery sky, broad ribbons around cacophonous pillars. I went with him, and so did other parts of me, that I'd lost, and we were the same, as much as we'd ever been. With one exception. Maybe father would miss me, but not for long: and mother wouldn't even know I was gone. Without me, there might not be any left of them, but maybe there would. Leaving made me sad, but I've never been able to cry without pretending, and no one heard. Now that I'd returned the rest of me, I had no reason to stay.

We broke apart on a cloud, and shape became different. Elongation and I spread into a straight line, hammered at by physics. At the last moment (it was white everywhere, or a color like it, that shone into thought, obscuring it) I remembered something—I'm not sure what: about who I was, where I was going, or something I had to do—but by then it didn't matter anymore. Wherever I went, I would still be there. Hopefully. And wherever that was, it was too late to turn back.

Hazily, in much the same manner as I had originally experienced it, I remembered a dream I'd had many times, before I'd had a self, before I'd lost it—or I thought it was a dream, but at that time it seemed a vision. I saw myself looking up from the base of a narrow tunnel, arms spread, rising into a pillar of white light so bright it bleached me from me; until I realized that the tunnel wasn't really narrow, nor a tunnel, but a well, gray bricks rising up the sides, leaking radiance: and at the top of that pillar was the sun, apotheosis and savior… I rose towards it, like water drawn from a deep river, absolutely weightless, timeless, unreal—shedding myself, shedding everything—past this place, the valley seen as chain and barrier, sight and absence of such; feeling that when I reached that point, like smoke rising within smoke, that separation would be complete, and wherever I went, effortless, I would drift calmly, within the sight of a clear seeing eye, as light over a tall hill on a beautiful, beautiful day.

The boy thought he was alone, but a girl came to him. She took his hand. Hers was cool, and smooth, and had much in it of goodness. In the late evening, she burned. They walked, and everywhere around them spread more flame, a radiant layer. Their footsteps came slowly and very quiet. They did not speak.

Rounding a hill, they saw, on the face of another, a group of three children, two boys and a girl. One had blond hair, the others brown. All were very young, unlike the others, who were not young at all. As they played, laughter came from them, the spare, uncaring tones of time suspended, lifting by blazing hands into high, secret winds.

Suddenly furious, the boy lifted a rock; threw it. He missed; it landed heavily, rolling. The three ceased to play. All turned their eyes to him: wide and startled, frightened. Their figures seemed caricatures in the dusk, angular in slenderness and blasphemy.

"Who do you think you are!" screamed the boy: stared at. "What right do you have? What reason?" But they said nothing—only turned away to run, their fright taking the place of all else, making it crude.

The boy moved forward, meaning to chase them. But if he had, the girl's hand would slip from his. Would she wait, or follow to the places he went? Surely the children ran quickly. They would break into pieces of themselves, hiding in more directions than anyone might follow. And even if he caught them, what could he do? That thing he craved (something that had once been his, but could be so no longer) could not be given, or taken, or made to change hands. He could not leave her here, and he wouldn't—and even if he had, there was nothing he could do.

The place in which they had played was very quiet.

::::::::::::::::::

Later that day, he sat by himself making music. Laura had gone. Perhaps he would see her again, perhaps not. The divided sky split beyond two.

This world did not move.

Knowing that, he wanted very badly to cry—and did.

ABOUT THE AUTHOR

Kyle Muntz is the author of *Voices* (Enigmatic Ink, 2010), *Sunshine in the Valley* (Civil Coping Mechanisms, 2011), and *VII* (Enigmatic Ink, 2012). He is interested in the literature of aesthetic and ideas.

8617547R0

Made in the USA
Lexington, KY
16 February 2011